Rumble Strips

Rumble Strips

Dylan Higgins

Decadal Press

Published by Decadal LLC
www.decadalpress.com

Paperback ISBN: 979-8-9916485-1-6
E-book ISBN: 979-8-9916485-0-9

Cover Design: Amy Wheeler, Design Wheel Graphics
Editing: Lynne Pearson, All That Editing

To Mom, my first beta reader

PART I

Chapter 1

A black town car made its way down a quiet Seattle city street as soft morning light streamed between buildings. The car pulled alongside the curb to a seven-story condo. Outside, a service man wearing a dark blue fleece jacket that read Belltown View Condos hosed down the sidewalk, a loyal green snake following him. He paused his spray as a freshly shaven man in his late twenties with black curly hair still wet from the shower exited the building. He greeted the service man and walked to the town car, his roller bag in tow spitting up water from the sidewalk that glistened in the morning sun.

The driver, a slender Ethiopian with a thin beard, exited the car and walked to the opened trunk. "Good morning, Jack," he said. The driver reached for the bag, a large golden cross visible in the open collar of his partially unbuttoned white shirt.

"Good morning, Negasi," the young man replied. He shook Negasi's hand and climbed into the back of the town car. Negasi shut the door behind him. Jack reached for a breath mint in the console tray and settled into the leather seat.

"How was the weekend?" Negasi asked.

"Got a chance to see the Mariners with my parents," he said.

"Did they win?"

"Afraid not," he said. "But it was nice to see my folks. I don't get to see them much with all of this traveling." He looked out the window as they pulled onto the Alaskan Way Viaduct. A ferry drifted away from Seattle toward Alki Beach, its white paint glowing in the morning light. Mount Rainier appeared in the southern sky, a pink tint across its summit.

"How many months has it been?"

"Six months for this project." He chomped on the mint, breaking it into pieces. "Six years if you count them all."

"I've appreciated your business."

"You've been a great find, Negasi. It took me a few years to find a reliable driver," he said, leaning over to grab a folded *Seattle Times* from the back pocket of the passenger seat. The headline read, "September 11 – One Year Later." He flipped through the pages, moving from tragedy remembered to ongoing onslaught in Afghanistan to obstinate recession across the globe.

By the time he was reading the box score for the Mariners, he had arrived at Sea-Tac International Airport. His bag stood waiting for him on the sidewalk. He wished Negasi a good week and headed to the security line.

"Please remove your boots," the security screener said, pointing to a pair of shiny black combat boots.

A pony-tailed man bent down, mumbling something to the floor.

Behind him, Jack slipped his Eccos off and swung his laptop up and into a plastic bin. He stood waiting, watching. The pony-tailed man tugged at his laces. Jack counted the eyelets, 12-14-16, and looked over his shoulder at the line building up behind him. The sum of nerves created a stagnant heat that hung in the air. An older man in a tweed hat and round eyeglasses caught Jack's eye.

"Welcome to the twenty-first century," the man said.

"Yeah, I still can't get used to this," Jack replied, peeking at his chrome watch and then at the boarding time on his ticket. Across from him, a woman dumped a small drugstore into a clear garbage bag, complaining as each container fell into a bed of plastic bottles.

"But I have to tell you, the wait is nothing compared to the germs," the spectacled man continued.

"The germs?" Jack said, his blue eyes narrowing.

"This screening area is richer than most of the Petri dishes back at my university lab."

Jack watched the combat boots land with a thud in the bin. Dirt clods broke off the soles and crumbled across the bin. "From the shoes, huh?"

"No, the feet. It's like a locker room floor in here. Fungus is crawling all over this floor."

Jack looked at the pony-tailed man's feet as he walked through the metal detector. His big toe poked through a hole in one of his gray wool socks. The toenail was yellow. "I didn't think anyone could make this more miserable."

"Sorry, young man," the old man said. "Tread lightly."

The agent ordered Jack to walk through the metal detector. Raising his arms, he felt newly exposed to the germs around him. He quickly slipped on his shoes and passed the pony-tailed man. The man mumbled to himself while digging his feet back into his boots, more dirt falling on the floor.

Jack glanced again at his watch. He would have time to get his coffee. He passed the long line at Starbucks and headed to Café Escape at the end of the terminal.

The barista recognized him. "The regular?"

"The regular," Jack nodded. The barista twisted to the drip coffee machine and poured a twenty-four-ounce cup. She handed it to Jack.

With the warm cup in hand, he settled into his favorite vinyl seat up against the window at gate B22. He sipped his coffee and watched dueling queues of passengers extend out from the counter in front of him.

"I've been taking this flight for the last six months," a sweating, bald man shouted as he leaned toward one of the gate agents. His stubby index finger stabbed the air. "And frankly, I'm sick and tired of a thirty-minute delay turning into two hours every goddamn week."

The gate agent absorbed his tirade. Clenching her jaw, she tightened the grip on the sides of the keyboard. A tree of tendons appeared on the back of her hands. "Sir, I'm sorry you're upset here, but there is nothing I can do. We are all learning the new rules as they continue to evolve," she explained. "Now, can you please stand to the side for a moment?"

"Do I have a choice?" The man shook his head, exhaling.

The gate agent picked up the handset. "Will Chicago-bound passenger Jack O'Neill please come to the ticket counter?" She scanned the line milling nervously in front of her.

Jack placed his coffee on the floor and walked up to the gate, boarding pass in hand.

"Mr. O'Neill?" the agent asked.

"Yes, ma'am," he said.

"It's your lucky day. We're going to be able to give you that first-class upgrade," she said, handing him a new boarding pass. "We'll be boarding in a few minutes."

He grabbed the new pass and slipped it into his shirt pocket, catching an envious glare from the bald man.

Back at his chair, he reached for a widowed *USA Today*. He scanned across the multicolored weather page and checked the weather forecast in Chicago. An early fall storm was in the forecast. He took another sip of his coffee and waited for his boarding call.

Hours later, Jack's plane touched down at O'Hare. As he walked down the left side of the moving sidewalk, he passed a family standing on the right, a harried-looking mother huddled over two small children. He quickly moved past and skipped off the belt as his Nokia phone rang, its monophonic tune a familiar beckon. A Chicago area code. He let it ring. No message icon. Relieved, he kept walking toward the rental car counter.

The phone rang again. Same number. "Damn it," he mumbled to himself, placing the phone to his ear and parking his bag.

"Hello, this is Jack,"

"Hi Jack, this is Ann. Have you arrived?"

"Just arrived," he said. "What's up?"

"Oh, great," she said. "I'm glad I caught you. The pre-production release crashed over the weekend, and we need a fix from your engineering team ASAP."

"Are Sarah and the team there?"

"Yes, they're working on it," she explained. "But I need you here to help calm the nerves of my executive team."

"Ok," Jack said. "I should be there by one p.m., Assuming traffic is agreeable."

"Thanks Jack," Ann replied. "See you soon."

Jack turned off his phone. He bounced it on his thigh and gritted his teeth. He passed a lonely metal sign before a set of sliding glass doors. The sign read No Return Beyond This Point. He exited the terminal as a gust of wind sent shivers down his back.

Chapter 2

Six years and one million frequent flier miles earlier, Jack O'Neill walked across the Martin Center stage at Gonzaga University's graduation ceremony. In his left hand he carried a diploma scribbled with Bachelor of Arts in Finance. As he waved his diploma and walked down the stairs, careful not to trip on his gown, he considered his next steps after college. Five weeks ago, three job offers lay on the desk before him. An offer to join an executive rotation program for a Portland-based bank, an offer for a finance analyst position at Ford, and an offer to become a technology consultant at an international consulting firm called Ascend Consulting. His diploma steered him into banking and finance, but the high-technology industry presented an allure he could not resist. The dot-com craze was emerging, and Jack joined the ranks of many graduates drawn into a fast-growing field.

After a summer spent on trains in Europe, Jack started with Ascend Consulting in the Seattle office. His first job was in the Bay Area. He was soon flying to San Francisco every week. He had an expense account. Reservations at four-star hotels. Per-diems. And, best of all, there was no homework, and the boss bought him drinks. He loved bragging to his friends, many still at university on the five-year plan.

As the projects piled up, so did the numbers. A savings account bulged to five figures. At first, he studied his statements, convinced the bank was overcounting. Later, he didn't even bother to open the envelope. As his frequent flier miles account grew, he mastered the arcane art of interpreting frequent flier award charts. He welcomed forty-hour weeks as mere vacations, sixty-hour weeks as leisurely strolls, and eighty-hour weeks as marathon tests of fortitude. Hours worked became badges of honor in the office.

Now holding elite status on several airlines, Jack made his way through the chilly O'Hare parking lot, passing long queues snaking out from every rental car counter. He continued straight to the preferred customer parking lot, where he selected the car of his choice as a reward for his loyalty. Scanning the parking lot like a kid in a candy store, he chose a new 2003 Chevy Blazer, jumped into the leather seat, and slammed the car from reverse into drive with the confidence of a company-insured driver. Passing over ominous spikes, he pulled the rental car into traffic and headed for Agora HQ.

Agora hired Ascend Consulting to retool the retail distribution conglomerate, moving its systems from bulky mainframes to the world wide web. The company was sold on the promise of selling its products on the internet, capitalizing on the technology wave that had reached the shores of every business.

Jack, recently promoted to project manager, turned into Agora's sprawling parking lot nestled in the suburbs west of Chicago. He left his bag in the back seat, swung the laptop bag over his shoulder, and walked through the full parking lot. Agora's logo, its name resting on a set of Greek columns, covered the glass entry. He swiped his badge at the sensor beside the double doors and entered the reception area. Two staircases framed the reception desk and curved up to a second story. Artificial plants were arranged across the lobby floor.

A heavyset woman dressed in a gray sweatshirt, blue jeans, and all-white athletic shoes paced back and forth on the second floor. She stopped at the top of the stairs and rested her hand on the railing.

"Good afternoon, Jack," she said, greeting him with a tight smile.

Ann was the first person he'd met at Agora. With twenty years of experience in IT, she had risen steadily from a customer service desk job to the lead manager of Agora's ambitious transformation strategy. She was Jack's client. Her intensity always reminded him of the championship-winning woman's basketball coach at Gonzaga.

"Afternoon, Ann," Jack responded mid-flight. "Do we have a fix yet?"

"Not yet," Ann said. "And I have a meeting at three p.m. with my VP."

"OK. Let me go meet with my team and get a status update," Jack said, "I can meet you in your office at two-thirty."

"Alright," Ann said, her eyes locked on Jack's. "It will be important to understand if this impacts the go-live date."

"Understood. See you at two-thirty ."

Each occupant of the individual offices he passed stared at the monitor in front of them, the outside world at their back. He wound deeper into the building, the walls seeming too narrow, the artwork more sporadic, the lights dimmer until he reached a windowless conference room. A flotilla of desktop computers surrounded by a sea of documents covered the conference room table. Like recently thrown confetti, yellow sticky notes lay scattered on the table, on screens, and crumpled on the floor. The rat-a-tat of keyboards emitted from the hands of a team locked into their monitors. A long sheet of white paper with columns stretched across multiple months and milestones marked by stars wallpapered one wall. On the other wall, scribbles, numbers, and graphs—the graffiti of business—covered different whiteboards. Jack stepped into the conference room.

"Hi, team."

"So glad you could join us," Sarah, the project lead, said, looking up from her keyboard with a smile. "Do you have some good news?"

"I'm afraid I was going to ask you the same," Jack responded. "Let's huddle up."

The team logged out of their computers, stood, and walked down the hall to a proper conference room. Sarah picked up an almost empty red cardboard box of cookies. She offered one to Jack, who picked through the remaining half-moons of chocolate chip cookies to find an untarnished peanut butter cookie. He quickly devoured it.

"Thanks, Sarah," he said, wiping a crumb from his lip. "I haven't had anything to eat since I landed."

"I figured. Can I grab you a coffee?"

"Sure," Jack said, reaching for the box of cookies. "I'll take this into the room."

He set the cookies on the table, asking, "Anyone looking for seconds?" Several team members surrounded the box and emptied it. "I'm waiting for Sarah to bring me a coffee, and then we'll get started."

"Before we jump in with work though, any good stories from the weekend?" Jack scanned the group, hoping to lighten the mood. Eyes darted away from his glance.

A younger man with wavy brown hair broke the silence. "I almost ended up as shark bait," he said, his words partially garbled by a mouth full of cookie. Gasps erupted across the table. Alex was the adventurous teammate based out of the San Francisco office. One week he was hanging by ropes from Half Dome; the next week he was swerving a mountain bike through Napa, but this was a first.

"Yeah, I was out at Stinson Beach, and it was an epic day of surfing. I'm out there eyeing the next wave, and all of sudden, I see a fin." His right hand went upright and swam forward. "I do a double take and then I see some of the other guys begin a steady paddle in."

"And you joined them, right?" Sarah asked as she walked into the room and handed Jack his coffee.

"Of course, I was right behind them. I think I was paddling in quicker than I surf."

"So did you go out later?" Jack asked.

"No way, I'm not that crazy. But the others were. They were back out there in no time. I decided to stay in. I didn't want to let you guys down by not showing up this week."

"Nice, Alex," Jack said, taking a sip of coffee. "I will note this dedication on your next performance review,"

"I'm trying sir."

"Well, if there aren't any other death-defying stories, let's get into it. I spoke with Ann as I entered the building," Jack told them. The conference room let out a collective sigh.

"She's eager to get an update on the fix. Do we have a root cause yet?"

"We are looking at the design docs, but it's going to take a while," Sarah explained. "Alex and I have double-checked the requirements and can't figure out why the order processing module failed. We think it has to do with the warehouse management system. We've sent an email to that team but haven't heard back."

"Ok, what does this mean for our launch date?" Jack responded, aware of Ann's earlier warning.

"This is critical path," Sarah replied. "We'll need this fixed by end of week to stay on track."

"Then let's get after it. I don't want to keep us all here for another weekend," he said.

The team rose from their seats and returned to their desks. Jack remained seated, watching them file out of the room.

The fifteen consultants, half of them from Chicago, the other half from spots across the country, had gelled nicely under his tutelage. Faced with the pressures of an aggressive timeline, a demanding client, and sacrificing summer weekends to the job, the team managed to stay close. Jack was the proud general who kept the troops well-fed, well-organized, and always clear on their mission: a relentless drive to launch.

Two piles of paper lay on the desk in front of him. On his right were test scripts to verify the system was ready for launch. On his left, a report confirming the development was finished and ready for testing.

The two piles were more than paper to Jack. They represented opposing armies ready to commence trench warfare. The developers were prepared to defend themselves against any defect discovered by the testing team. The testers, in turn, were ready to bang the design specifications on the table and explain, beg, and finally insist that the system work a particular way. As this tit-for-tat flared, Jack knew it was on his shoulders to manufacture an armistice—an armistice that convinced both parties to put down their weapons and focus on the project objectives.

He took a deep breath and flipped nervously through each pile. Forming a temporary truce, he combined the piles and balanced them on his right forearm. He got up out of his chair and left the room to enter the trenches.

Chapter 3

"A nice day to leave Seattle. Looks like it's going to rain all day," Negasi said as he put the car in gear and pulled from the curb. "How's Chicago been treating you?"

"As good as can be expected. Last week we started the testing. If everything goes well, I should be back in Seattle on a more permanent basis in the next month or so. Of course, nothing's stopping them from shipping me off someplace else. How's school going for you ?"

"I'm going to be graduating here in two more quarters," Negasi said.

"No more taxicabs for you," Jack remarked. "Any job opportunities lined up yet?"

"Not yet. I'll start the process soon though," he said. "I'm not spending all of this money to be driving this for the rest of my life." He nodded dismissively at raindrops collecting on the dashboard.

"Let me know if you need any help. We could always use a smart, motivated electrical engineer from U-Dub."

"Thanks, sir. I appreciate it," Negasi said.

"I haven't seen any recent news from Ethiopia." Jack set down the newspaper on the seat beside him.

"Our Prime Minister Meles," Negasi began. "Do you remember me telling you about him?"

"Yes, he's the one who led the guerrilla war against the Marxists." Six months of trips to Sea-Tac meant Jack was well-versed in East African politics.

"Good memory, sir," Negasi said. "Well, I'm still nervous about his support for democratic reforms, but he's done a great job at getting the economy on strong footing."

"That's a good start."

"You're right. It's a good start. The problem is that they are asking us to open our financial markets to the world."

"And remove barriers to foreign investments?"

"Correct, sir. The World Bank playbook."

"Sounds like it," Jack said. "I took an international economics class in college."

"Then you will understand that I'm a little nervous about opening the Ethiopian markets. Eighty-five percent of our economy is rural and dependent on bank financing. Any crazy swings in the markets could get us in a lot of trouble. When Kenya liberalized in the early '90s, it was disastrous. Unfortunately, our position against liberalization has caused the IMF to suspend aid."

"That can't be good," he said, catching Negasi's dark eyes in the rearview mirror.

"No, it's terrible. Many of us support Meles and we're hoping the liberalization slows down. My brother owns a coffee farm and is feeling the pinch. The coffee markets are already at record lows, and he's afraid he'll never survive if they move too fast."

"Probably an uphill battle," Jack said. "I'm afraid those DC folks can be pretty set in their ways. But it's worth trying."

"That's all we can do, sir. Just keep trying to make our voices heard."

"Keep it up, Negasi," Jack said. The car pulled into the departure drop-off areas. "Thanks again and enjoy the week. Mind if I take the paper?"

"Not at all, sir," Negasi said, waving him along.

After a surprisingly short trip through security, Jack made a beeline for Café Escape.

"A cup of the regular drip to go, please," Jack said while flipping absentmindedly through the newspaper.

"Excuse me? What kind?" the barista asked sharply.

"The regular," Jack said curtly.

"Are you sure?" she challenged again.

He looked up, not recognizing the unfamiliar voice.

A woman near his age stood waiting expectantly. Her head slanted to one side, olive eyes observing him. Her slightly disheveled sandy-brown hair burst from the top of her head and cascaded across her army green shirt. He noticed a necklace of white seashells framed against her tanned skin. She was several inches shorter than Jack, but her presence made him feel smaller. He felt blood rush to his cheeks. His grip on the newspaper loosened. Something untethered inside him.

"Are you sure?" she asked a second time. This time, more slowly. She wiped her hand across a white apron smudged with coffee grounds.

He grabbed his United Airlines credit card, seeking the comfort of its sharp edges, the status it entailed grounding him to his constructed confidence. "Yep," he said, handing her the card. "Sure enough that I get it every week."

"OK, fine," she said, taking the card. "But you won't need this if you get a cup of the Fair Trade Tropical." She twisted the card playfully between her slender fingers. He noticed the soft curve of her cuticles. Her smile framed by two deep dimples. He was unmoored again.

"Listen, I'm sorry, but I've got to catch a flight," he pleaded with her.

"You sure?" she responded, the card maintaining its dance in her fingers.

"Alright, what do you want me to drink?"

"How 'bout a cup of the Tropical?" She handed his credit card back to him. "And you don't need this. It's my treat."

"If it's free, why not?" He shrugged and slipped the card back into his wallet. When he looked up again, she was dispensing his coffee. A strand of hair split from its relatives and fell across her face. Her bottom lip extended, and with a quick burst, she blew the hair back in place. She turned to Jack.

"Every Monday?" she asked.

"Excuse me?" Jack looked up to catch her eye.

"You commute every Monday?'

"Yep. And are you the new Monday barista?"

"That's right. I'm working Mondays now." She placed his coffee on the counter. "I'm Hope. What's your name?" She extended her hand.

"Jack. Jack O'Neill." He met her hand. He wasn't sure if the warmth of her hand was from the coffee or her body. The feeling seemed to stay in his hand as he retracted it. He hesitated before turning to the terminal.

"Your parents hippies?"

"You need to ask?"

"Every Monday, huh?" A slight grin appeared on his face.

"Every Monday." She nodded.

A last call announcement for Flight 374 to Chicago blared from the airport's speakers.

"That's me," Jack said. "This better be good." He lifted the cup toward Hope and turned to punch the button on his bag. A handle sprung into his waiting hand. He merged into the concourse traffic and took a sip of the Tropical.

It was delicious. He swished the coffee between his teeth. The earthy and sweet tones were a sharp contrast to his regular, acidic cup. He looked back to Hope. She was taking a folded twenty-dollar note from a pilot but watching Jack. His head cocked, his chin extended, he nodded in approval. She winked and turned away to get the pilot's drink.

Jack continued to frogger his way to his gate and onto his flight. He plopped into his seat. His thoughts moved to the week ahead. He took an especially large sip of coffee, taking in the chocolate aroma. Seattle's raindrops were accumulating on the plane's window. They reminded him of seashells.

Chapter 4

Absent a crisis, the first meeting of each week was the executive planning meeting. Jack sat near the head of the table where Ann was waiting for the attendees to find seats. Her index finger tapped the table as if she was sending Morse code. She flipped through her notes.

"I hope everyone had a great weekend," she said as the last person snuck into the conference room balancing a cup of coffee while gently closing the door. "I want to again thank you all for your hard work last week getting the finishing touches on the system. Jack, I'd especially like to thank your team for putting in a long week to get the customer module finished. I know all of us here at Agora appreciate your team's work.

"Now, let me remind everyone that we must keep the momentum going. It's been a long six-month marathon, and the finish line is in sight."

Ann reviewed the status with each of her team leads. She turned to Jack last. "Is your development team ready to turn the last of their code over to testing today?"

"Yes," he responded. "We had a final code review last Friday and we're set to go. I'll coordinate with everyone after this meeting."

"Excellent. If there is anything we can do to help you, let me know," she replied, pausing. "And one other thing. I realize most of your team is from out of town, and they usually leave early on Friday. But I'm asking some of the Agora folks to work extra-long hours here this week, so I expect the same from your team."

"Not a problem. We were already planning for the crunch," Jack said, surprised Ann mentioned this yet again. Jack had hinted to her that many of his teammates spent long hours at the office over the weekend, often unproductive when Agora full-time employees were no-shows. Having to assuage his team members' frustrations about their hours was tough enough, and he didn't need it from the client side as well.

"Great," Ann said, straightening her papers and slamming them against the table. "Then, if there isn't anything else, let's get back to work. Thanks, everyone."

Jack stood and walked into the routine of another week. On Mondays, the team would regroup for the week ahead. Even when the client threw a curveball in a Monday session, he felt it was his job to soften the message and motivate his team. By Monday evening, he wanted them to be clear on their direction. Tuesdays through Thursdays were the most grueling. The team focused on its deliverables for the week, eager to reduce the risk of weekend work. Days often evolved into late evenings, and by the time the team disbursed, the caravan of Ascend cars were the only ones left in the parking lot. If the team managed to meet its targets by Friday, half would catch a flight home, and the other half would leave early to return to their homes in the Chicago area.

By Thursday of this week, Jack's team was on schedule, and they went to a dinner at Gibson's Steakhouse in the Loop. A well-dressed waiter led the group of fifteen to a private room at the back of the restaurant. A long table was elegantly set with crystal wineglasses. Flared napkins begged for warm laps. Beside wide white plates, sets of knives, forks, and spoons formed a stairway of utensils. The dark mahogany panels and crisp white tablecloths suggested the specialty of the house: seared filet mignons and garlic-mashed Yukon golds.

A highlight of any project, team dinners were a chance to pursue the adage of working hard and playing harder. An open invitation to order anything on the menu. Eyes would lock onto the right side of the menu, secretly scanning the escalating prices as the team members swept down like vultures to the most expensive item. Surf and Turf was a popular choice at these dinners.

As the team placed their orders, the conversations began. While the drinks had not yet taken effect, the focus of the table shifted to Jack as he answered questions ranging from the size of this year's raises to the state of the consulting business. Eventually, however, the alcohol kicked in, and casual chatter displaced business-speak.

Jack sat back in his chair, happy to no longer be the center of attention. He listened as the team analyzed the odds of a Bears victory. Sipping his hefeweizen, he scanned the room and swelled with pride like a proud parent of an honor roll student. He was proud of the diverse team he had assembled. Proud that they'd remained productive through the long hours and tense moments.

But his pride turned to dejection when he remembered the look on their faces after hearing about Ann's latest pushes. He somehow felt responsible for the torture his team had endured the past few months. It was not visible in his public persona. Years of tough clients and gut-wrenching decisions had built a coat of armor around his soul. Inside, however, guilt tore at his pride. He was happy to see the waiter bringing his filet mignon, rescuing him from any risk of an accidental display of uncertainty.

After everyone had politely refused but then ordered dessert, Jack paid for the meal, earning another couple thousand frequent flier miles.

"You guys interested in going out for some more drinks?" Jack asked as he rose from his seat. Some of the team squirmed in their chairs. "Oh, and for those of you who want to go to the gym, meet up with significant others, or do things that are rumored to go on outside of work, you're free to do those as well."

Of course, it was too late. Even voluntary socializing with the boss somehow became mandatory. As he slipped the neatly folded receipt into his wallet, his team followed their Pied Piper out the door. Jack was happy to delay the return to his stale, lonely corporate apartment.

They ducked into the first martini bar that got them out of the windy night. The team invaded the leather couches spread randomly across the floor in the back room of the bar. Sarah sat down on a couch next to Jack.

She turned to him. "So, Mr. Manager. How was the filet mignon?"

"Succulent," Jack responded, kissing the tips of his fingers, and splaying them out.

"Well, I'll second that. Nothing quite beats Gibson's. Especially when the company's paying for it."

"You're right about that one."

A bow-tied waiter stopped by their couch. "What are you two having?" he asked Jack.

"Sarah?" Jack turned to her.

"I'll have a Chocolate Martini," she replied.

"And I'll have a hefeweizen," Jack said. The waiter returned to the bar. "How's Dmitri doing?" Jack asked.

"Big news," she said, smiling. "He asked me to move in with him this weekend."

"Congratulations," Jack said, putting his hand to his ears. "Are those wedding bells I hear."

"Be quiet, will you," she said, shooing away his comment with a wave.

"I'm only kidding. I'm just jealous, you know. Living in the same town as your partner. Wouldn't that be nice?"

"You're not seeing anyone these days?"

"Afraid not, I haven't had a serious girlfriend since I got promoted. Ironic, isn't it?" He raised his eyebrows.

"I'm sure you'll find someone. You're a good catch."

"Ha, if you can catch me. All this traveling wears you down."

The waiter arrived, set two napkins gently on the glass table, and placed the drinks on them.

"Go ahead and open up a tab," Jack said.

"I was hoping you'd say that," the waiter said. "Everyone else has been pointing at you when I asked how they wanted to pay."

"Go figure," Jack replied, handing the waiter his credit card, and looking across the room to the raised glasses of his thankful team. He raised his own glass in return.

"Sarah, I hate to bring up work," Jack said. "But I was wondering…"

"What's on your mind, Jack?"

He took a long gulp from his hefeweizen and sat back on the leather couch. "Well, what is the morale of the team like right now. I feel like I'm spending so much time massaging the client's ego, I don't know how my own team is doing."

"Don't get me wrong, it hasn't been easy the past few weeks, but I think we're standing strong."

"Nobody's talking about quitting?"

"Not openly, at least. I took a couple of my team members out to lunch this week and gave them a pep talk and they're keeping their heads up."

"That's great to hear," Jack said.

"Can I ask you something about work?"

"What's that?"

"Have you had a chance to talk with Michael about my promotion to manager?"

"I have," Jack said. Michael, the managing partner, had approved her promotion only yesterday.

"And?" She moved closer on the couch.

"You've done a great job this year."

"And?"

"Your prospects are very good."

"And?"

"Well..." Jack said, pausing.

Sarah froze.

"Well, I can't tell you quite yet," Jack said. "You'll have to hear from Michael when they make the promotion announcements next month."

"Any hints?"

"I've already given you plenty," Jack protested. "Now, let's stop talking about work. What are you and Dmitri planning for this weekend?" He didn't want anything more to slip out.

"I think he's got tickets to the Bears."

"Bears, Packers. That should be a fun one," Jack said. He saw himself watching the game on TV back in Seattle.

"What do you have planned?" Sarah asked.

"I was just thinking that," he said. "I don't have anything planned yet."

"Jack! Sarah!" Alex interrupted, yelling from across the room. He had assembled the rest of the team against the bar. "You guys ready for some tequila shots?"

"I think we're fine," Jack said, knowing his stomach was sufficiently lubed.

"Speak for yourself," Sarah rose and joined the group. She extended her hand to Jack and pulled him up from the couch. "You too, boss."

A couple of rounds later, the group was shooed from the dance floor and out into the crisp autumn night. A fleet of taxis rounded the corner and headed in their direction.

"The first one is for the Oak Park people," Jack said as some of his team lined up to get into the taxi.

Sarah was one of them. Before she bent down to get in, she turned to Jack and hugged him warmly, thanking him. She closed the door behind her, and the taxi drove off, its tailpipe coughing exhaust into the sky.

The rest of the group piled into the other taxis. Some were off to apartments nearby in the Loop and others, like Jack, back to corporate apartments in the western suburbs.

When Jack arrived at his apartment, he opened the door and scanned the room. A scarlet couch, a TV, and cream-colored kitchen cabinets. The only signs of life were a stack of dishes in the sink and a bath towel over a dining chair. He ransacked his cupboards, scavenging for a late-night snack. He found old tortilla chips and cut around the mold from a block of cheddar. He prepared nachos, sat down on the couch, and turned on the TV. He flipped through *Seinfeld* re-runs and *Sportscenter* highlights and drifted to sleep. He woke up to Ron Popiel offering him a ShowTime Rotisserie Oven and moved into his bedroom, stepping over the open roller bag that served as his closet. He pulled back the cover, dropped onto the bed, and reached for the extra pillow to hold against his body.

As he drifted to sleep and held the pillow closer, he felt himself running in the dark night, sweat pouring down his forehead. His lungs inhaled the cold, moist air. When he looked around, he recognized the place as the jogging trail at Green Lake back in Seattle. He could make out the orange blur of distant streetlights, the dark outlines of trees, and his own breath chugging like a locomotive. A torrential downpour made the sidewalk glisten. He could hear repetitive slaps of shoes nearby but could not see them anywhere. Suddenly, a group of three women, all wearing hooded sweatshirts, appeared, blocking the path. Jack swerved off the pavement onto the muddy bank and into a puddle. The water splashed violently and covered his legs. A cacophony of giggles snuck out from under the hoods of the joggers. Catching the glance of one of them, he thought he made out the dimpled smile of Hope. She turned and kept running before he could stop her.

He woke with his lips glued to the pillow. He wiped his mouth with his forearm, pulled the covers over his legs, and pulled the pillow closer. He fell fast asleep.

Chapter 5

"What perspective do you take?" Jack asked Negasi. Their car had stopped at the 1st Ave Bridge. The drawbridge was up. Jack looked out the window at the drivers in the cars next to him. Their necks craning to see if they would make out the size of the boat passing in the waterway below, calculating their delay. Their stress weighed him down.

"What do you mean, sir?" Negasi asked.

"What keeps you working so hard?"

"It all depends on priorities. I came to this country because of the opportunities I didn't have in Ethiopia," Negasi said. "And now that I'm here, I have a wife and a child. My priorities are with them. Every morning, I wake up and do what I do for them."

"What about before that?" Jack persisted. "When you were single?"

"Those were the days, sir," Negasi said. "Every day was another day to experience America. A chance to make it on my own."

"Did you ever get tired of it?"

"Physically tired, sure." Negasi nodded. "But I was trying to survive day to day. I couldn't rest. I worked in parking lots. I worked in Ethiopian restaurants. I saved here, I saved there. When I wrote to my mom to tell her I was accepted at the UW, I wrote carefully, in my best writing. I knew she would take the letter and walk the streets back home waving it as proof that America is the land of dreams."

"I'm sure she was proud," Jack said. "We are lucky here, Negasi. There is no doubt about that."

"Yes, sir," Negasi said. "For all of its faults, this place still provides much opportunity."

The town car rounded its way into the Sea-Tac departure lane, and Jack stepped onto the curb. He passed through security, the conflict wrestling in his head. In one corner the aspirations and dreams of Negasi. In the other, Jack's expectations and drive that powered him all these years, disconnected from any purpose beyond the drive itself.

He turned the corner and headed toward his gate and Café Escape. She was there. Today, her hair tied back in a ponytail. The seashell necklace more prominent. It rested on the rolling hills of her clavicle. She reached for someone's credit card, and he noticed a pair of friendship bracelets on her right wrist. He quickened his pace to join the queue, watching her behind the counter the whole time. When her eyes finally met Jack's, he blushed again.

"Just a second. Just a second. I'll remember," she said. Her index finger bounced in front of him. "Jack! Right? And you get a cup of Tropical."

"If it's free, sure."

"Sorry, Charlie. Not this time. But please don't tell me you're going back to the regular," she said, her palms touching each other, forming a prayer.

"The Tropical is like twice the price, though."

"It's twice the flavor," she responded. "But, more importantly, why sacrifice a pause in your hectic life with a homogenized, corporatized, dehumanized, commoditized, poorly tasting cup of the regular drip."

"Half-price, and I'll buy it," he said, pulling out his credit card.

"Nice try," she replied. She looked over Jack's shoulder. A line was forming. "Are you really going to disappoint me?"

"How could I?" Jack turned around to see the line. "Make it a Tropical. A large."

"Wonderful," she said, pirouetting on one foot. "A grande it is." She poured his coffee and swiped his card. "You're one of the good ones, Jack."

"You mean your tactics don't work on everyone?" He moved aside to allow the line to move forward.

"Not always," she said.

Jack shook his head. He sipped the coffee, its aroma again overwhelming him with unfamiliar flavors. He checked his boarding pass. He had time to spare.

"What's the secret behind this stuff?" he asked Hope.

"You really want to know?"

"That's why I'm still here."

"Really? Okay, one second." Hope turned to a colleague. "Frankie, can you take the register for a minute?" At his nod, she moved to the side to continue their conversation.

"The secret? I like to believe it is the origins."

"Origins? You mean where it's from," Jack said.

"Yep."

"And where would that be."

She stared at a framed photo of a coffee plantation nestled at the foot of a massive volcano. "It is a place where rumbling volcanoes tickle the sky, serene lakes lie in the hills, rain bathes all that is green, and the sun warms the soil."

"Sounds like heaven on earth," he responded. "Where is this place?"

"Guatemala."

"Guatemala, huh?" He raised an eyebrow. "Don't know much about it. But I agree, they can sure make a damn good cup of coffee."

"I wouldn't steer you wrong now, would I?"

Jack stayed leaning against the bar. He took a couple sips of his coffee and watched Hope bounce knowingly around the space. He checked his boarding pass and watch again. Time slowed for him.

"So, Hope," he said, "I just don't get it. How does someone like you find yourself working at a café at an airport?"

"Two reasons," she said, giving the peace sign.

"First, there is no place in the city where I can be so close to the wonders of the world. It's possible to walk over to a ticket agent, buy a ticket, skip to the gate, and be whisked away to a new world in a few hours. The possibilities are endless. I even carry this every day, just in case." She pulled out a tattered passport and waved it like a Bible in the hand of a fire and brimstone preacher.

"And the second?"

"The second is my appreciation for what airports represent today. This airport is a meeting place for diverse cultures. In ancient times, the new ideas emerged from street markets. Just think of Marco Polo's caravan passing from market to market."

Jack nodded as he remembered his middle school history teacher dragging his finger across the wall-sized world map.

"To me," Hope continued, "airports are the place where cultures and their ideas intermingle at a mind-boggling pace. I'm lucky enough to be serving coffee and absorbing it all," she said, spreading her hands across the bottles of flavored syrup lined between Jack and her.

As one hand passed near him, he caught a new aroma. It smelled of peaches. He breathed deeply. "I never thought someone could come up with a convincing reason to work here, but, by God, you've managed to do it."

"You're talking to an eternal optimist. There isn't much I can't do without attempting to put a positive spin on it," she said. "Despite the way the world seems to be going sometimes."

"That's admirable," Jack replied. "And a good way to deal with people like me. Those of us always in a rush. Always with someplace to go."

"You shouldn't lump yourself with them. You stopped. You listened. You don't have to accept my rants. But, by listening, you're doing much more than the others." She rested her bare arm gently on the spouts of the syrup bottles. The muscles in her arms slightly flexed, she leaned into Jack as if she had a secret to share.

"You won't believe how many people I watch pass through this café who are running but they don't know why. Before they know it, they have lived a life of plans," she said.

"I don't think that's entirely fair, Hope," Jack said. "Some of them are only trying to support their families."

"Of course they are. But many are caught up in something else."

"And what's that?" Jack inquired cynically.

She waved at the shops lining the airport concourse. "Madison Avenue has convinced them that certain products will bring them happiness. To them, it's an easy calculation: more money equals more goods equals more happiness. They jump on the treadmill, choose the program marked Sprint, and before they know it the sons and daughters of misplaced priorities—greed and want—are born. They continue sprinting until they've become completely desensitized to their surroundings."

Jack was breathless. He hadn't heard an impassioned sermon like that since college. The final boarding call for his flight was announced over the loudspeaker.

He wanted to stay and hear her out. To test her assumptions. To stretch her theory. To probe her motivations. Instead, he pulled back his cuff and looked at his watch. "Speaking of being in a rush…"

"You have to catch your flight to Chicago," Hope said. "I know Jack. I'm sorry for the rant. I don't usually get this excited."

"You don't expect me to believe that one, do you?" He slid his empty cup Tropical down to her. "You are an amazing woman."

"And you are a great customer," Hope said. "Now, go get 'em, Tiger." She punched Jack squarely on the shoulder. He smelled peaches again.

"After that speech, I'm not sure how to go get 'em."

"You'll figure it out."

"Thanks, Hope," Jack said and ran toward his gate. He felt light-headed and dazed as he sprinted past his fellow travelers. He rubbed his arm where Hope had hit him. He wondered if it would bruise. It would be a nice reminder.

Chapter 6

The week passed quickly. The team in a groove. Open warfare between factions of engineers, testers, and uneasy clients temporarily averted. Each party content to stay in their camp, drawn out only by morning treats or evening drinks.

Jack rescheduled and caught an earlier flight back to Seattle. Upon arriving, he headed directly to Café Escape. Hope was busy conducting the impatient traffic behind the counter, directing them into a line out of the café and along the terminal wall. He waited on the other side. The crowds hurried past. He watched Hope from afar, building his courage to cross the stream of passengers.

When the line died down, and Hope left the counter to wipe down empty tables, Jack made his move.

He cleared his throat. "Is this table taken?"

"Jack!" she said, a smile forming between two dimples. She slid a chair out from under the table and pivoted it toward Jack. Grabbing the towel wrapped around her forearm, she quickly wiped the seat clean. "It's all yours. And if you give me a minute, I can join you on my break."

She walked back to the counter, dropped the towel in the sink, and returned. She sat across from Jack and blew a strand of hair from her face.

"Didn't expect to see you here," she said, exhaling lightly. "How was your week?"

"Great. How was yours?"

"Also, great. We had an unusually warm week. Can I get you something?"

"No thanks. But I've got something else you could do for me." Jack paused. He swallowed, preparing himself for the ask. "I was wondering. Do you have anything going on this weekend?"

"Not really." Her eyes narrowed, a mischievous grin slowly formed. "And why might you ask?"

"Well," he said. "I was just thinking of getting outside a bit."

Hope nodded and nodded, tugging at the anticipated question.

"I was thinking maybe we could enjoy this nice weather someplace," he said quickly.

"That sounds great. What are you thinking?"

"I haven't been on a hike for years. You like hiking?"

"I love it. I can even recommend a spot. Just off I-90 there's a beautiful waterfall."

"Sounds good to me. Do you work tomorrow?"

"Luckily, I've got the day off."

"Eight a.m.?"

"You got it." She grabbed a pen from her apron and jotted something on a napkin. "Here's my address. See you then."

"Great." He folded the napkin and placed it in his back pocket. "Looking forward to it."

"Rest those legs," Hope said, "see you tomorrow." She returned to the counter. A female coworker whispered something to Hope, and they giggled.

Jack walked to the exit. His roller bag seemed a bit lighter, maneuvering between crowds more enjoyable. He picked the napkin from his back pocket and unfolded it. There was an address, a phone number, and a smiley face.

At eight a.m., he turned left off Olive Way down Summit Ave and arrived at Hope's apartment complex tucked between two large, thinning maple trees. Piles of leaves lay along the sidewalk. Dressed in a brown fleece jacket, green cargo pants, and a pumpkin orange beanie, she was waiting at the top of the stairs. Seeing Jack, she slung a matching orange backpack over one shoulder and skipped down the stairs, carrying two coffee travel mugs in one hand. Setting them on the roof of Jack's black Audi sedan, she opened the door.

"You know, I was going to suggest we stop for some coffee," he said.

"That's okay," she replied, sitting down, and handing one travel mug to Jack. "The coffee from work often travels home with me."

"Not going to complain." He grabbed the mug and took a sip. "Delicious. What a way to start the day." He pulled the car from the curb, and they headed west up into the Cascades. "Off we go." He accelerated down Summit Ave.

Forty-five minutes later, he exited I-90 and wound along a paved two-lane road that quickly deteriorated into a dirt logging road. A short, bumpy ride later, a brown wooden signpost stood on the side of the road. A stick figure with a hiking stick in hand and a yellow arrow pointed to the beginning of the trail. They stuffed apples, trail mix, and two water bottles into Hope's orange backpack. Jack's offer to shoulder the pack was politely rebuffed and they dropped off the road onto the trail.

The trail followed the highway for the first mile. The incessant, predictable sounds of passing cars drowning out the whispers of Mother Nature.

Jack followed Hope deeper into the forest. She set a fast pace, stepping confidently ahead. The path steepened, and he found himself short of breath. The stair machines at the gym, each movement calculated, and every step precise, were no match for the exposed roots and rocks of the trail. The forest thickened as they climbed, and the dew from the trees around them hung in the air, dropping the temperature. The suggestive melodies of a trickling creek and a chance encounter with a startled Northern Flicker replaced the sounds of the now-distant highway. They followed the creek to a larger stream and the loud rush of whitewater.

Hope turned to him. "Almost there. It's just around the bend."

"My heart thanks you," he said.

The trail dead ended. A large boulder lay on one side of the trail. Down below, a tall waterfall emerged from the forest and tumbled to a pool beneath it. Steep, moss-covered walls encircled the pool. Mist rose from the water in puffs.

Jack sat on a wide, moss-covered rock. Hope removed the backpack and fished out a water bottle, offering it to him.

He unscrewed the cap and took a large gulp of water. "That was a good climb. My legs are feeling it."

"Going down will be much easier." She took a large bite of an apple. "Thanks for suggesting this."

"You're welcome. I've enjoyed our chats at the café, but they're always so rushed."

She bowed slightly. "Glad to be of service. It's nice that you listen."

"I especially loved to hear your perspective on the airport. It was so refreshing." He grabbed a handful of trail mix. He stared at the raisins, almonds, and M&Ms in his palm. "I wanted to ask you about the coffee."

"What about it?"

"How did you get so passionate about it?"

"Great question," she said, placing her apple on one knee. "A few years back, 1999 to be precise, I was in between jobs and looking for a fresh perspective. I applied for a fellowship with a non-profit called Coffee Connect, and they sponsored a trip to Guatemala. I ended up spending three months down there at this fascinating place called Nueva Amanecer or New Dawn."

"What made it fascinating?" Jack asked, taking another handful of trail mix.

"A group of ex-combatants from the Guatemalan civil war started it. As part of the 1996 Peace Accords, they were offered a coffee plantation. A coffee plantation where they could apply the cooperative principles they spent over thirty years fighting for. I just loved the people and the opportunity to help."

"Have you been back since?"

"I haven't. God willing, I will someday. They are such wonderful people."

"And how did you end up at the café?"

"When I returned from Guatemala, I started taking night classes at Seattle Community College. I was looking to get a certificate in non-profit management. While I was attending, I took the job at the café. Once I got the certificate, no job materialized, so I just fell into working more hours at the café. I'll find something eventually."

"I'm sure you will."

She took another bite of her apple. "What about you? How did you end up commuting by airplane?"

Jack stared out at the waterfall in the distance. "Well, I've been at this job since I graduated in 1995. It sometimes feels like it's been pre-ordained that I would end up in business in some capacity. I was head of my high school investing club, I studied finance in college, and it seemed natural to take a consulting job."

"You enjoy it?"

"I think so," he said. "It's intellectually stimulating, and I enjoy the people I work with."

"And you get to travel, right?"

"Not sure I would call it travel, feels more like an extended commute."

"You got to meet me, right?"

"Well, that's turning out to be a pleasant surprise." He raised one eyebrow.

"I'm glad I'm pleasant."

"Very, it turns out."

She blushed slightly and took a final bite of her apple. They both sat silent, watching the waterfall below.

A group of hikers joined them. Hope jumped up and offered to take their photo. Jack would have never thought to ask.

The group left, and he turned to Hope. "We have to do this again," Jack said.

"I'd like that," she said. "You know where to find me."

"Your apartment or your café?"

"Slow down there, Jack. The café for now."

"Okay," he said, "for now."

He looked over at her. She gave him a mischievous grin.

They both turned back to the rushing water. A stick twirled in the gently swirling pool above the waterfall. It lodged against a rock, bouncing from the surge of the stream.

It broke loose and tumbled down into the whitewater below.
At the mercy of the stream, the stick was lost from sight.

33

Chapter 7

Jack stretched his arms and looked out the town car window. "Negasi, what made you finally leave?"

"Ethiopia?"

"Yeah, Ethiopia?"

"That's a good question," he said, looking in his side mirror as he switched from the fast lane to the slow lane. "I had been thinking about leaving for some time. My family was a target during the civil war. I was torn between two desires: a desire to stay home and fight and a desire to start a family somewhere else."

"But, by leaving, wouldn't you be leaving your family behind?"

"Yes and no. Family members were always trying to get out. And my mother was insistent that I leave as well. Of course, the more she pushed, the more I wanted to stay." Negasi sighed and gazed out at the passing homes. The town car swerved out of its lane and shook like a braking locomotive.

"Oh, sorry, sir," Negasi said as he corrected his course. "I guess it was finally something like those rumble strips back there that did it."

"Rumble strips? Is that what those grooves on the side of the highway are called?"

"Yes, rumble strips. See sir. We all get into our routines in life. We're in cruise control, and we forget that we are driving. We have decisions to make. Roads to turn down. I kept putting off a decision. Then, one day, a letter came from my cousin. He wrote of his new Ethiopian restaurant, his wife, and his new home in Seattle. I used to dream about all these things when I kicked around a football back home. In Seattle, he was living that dream, and I knew I had that chance as well.

I just needed someone to remind me that it was time to turn down a new road. I needed a rumble strip to wake me up."

"And are you glad you did it?"

"Yes, but it was the most difficult decision of my life. Only two years after I left, my mother was killed. I regret not being there with her. But if I was over there, I would have never met Winnie. She's been my savior."

"Well, I'm sure as hell glad you came here."

"Thank you, sir," Negasi replied. "By the way, are you heading to a new city this morning or just taking an earlier flight?"

"Nope, I just want some more time at the airport," Jack said nonchalantly.

"You? More time in the airport? That doesn't seem right." Negasi shook his head.

"Yeah, I just need some time to talk with someone," Jack said as a hint of a grin appeared.

"Oh, I see, sir. You've found yourself another one of those flight attendants, huh?" he said as his eyes met Jack's in the rearview mirror.

"No, not a flight attendant, but someone who works at one of the coffee shops at the airport," Jack said, "She's a fun one."

Negasi studied him through the mirror. "I can see something in your eyes. You like this one, Jack."

"We'll see Negasi, we'll see."

Jack's good intentions ran into bad luck when he reached Café Escape. He got his Tropical from Hope, but she was slammed with customers. He spent the time alternating between the newspaper and watching her gracefully handle the onslaught. She blew her hair out of her face every few seconds. The hair on the side of her head darkened as he caught glimpses of sweat forming around her temples. She looked at him with a slight exhale, her lips rounding to a pout. He felt an urge to kiss them.

When he reached the bottom of his Tropical, he realized he wasn't going to have a good conversation with her. He walked up to the counter.

"Hey, I've got to run," he said.

"Oh, Jack, I'm so sorry." She closed her hands together. "Please, please call me this week so we can chat."

"I will. I definitely will. Good luck with the crowd."

"And Jack, thanks again for the hike. I liked that a lot," she yelled as he walked past the long line of customers on his way to his flight.

"No problem, we'll have to do it again," he said. A young man in line nodded in approval to Jack. Jack smiled back at him.

Upon arriving in Chicago, he called Sarah.

She answered with a flustered voice. "Jack, I have some bad news. Ann noticed over the weekend that our developers were using the wrong revision of the design document for part of the customer module."

"Are you kidding?" Jack groaned in disbelief. "How the hell could that happen?"

"Who knows? They could have checked the wrong version of the document out of the database," Sarah explained. "Does this mean we'll have to postpone the testing?"

"You betcha. At least until we can have the developer reprogram the module," Jack said.

"Yuck. It's not going to be a fun week, huh?"

"That's an understatement. In fact, we're probably going to have part of the team stay here over the weekend."

"Really?"

"I hate doing it," Jack said. "But Ann is breathing down our necks right now. Our latest bill caused an uproar. They want results. Soon."

"Well, I can stay behind," Sarah offered.

"Thanks, Sarah. I'll need the company."

"You don't have to stay, Jack," she said. "Every other time we've stayed behind, you've volunteered."

"It goes with the job," he replied. "I'm used to it. The others though, I'm not so sure. Can you have someone order lunch for our team meeting? It should help soften the blow."

"Sure."

"And don't forget drinks."

"Stiff ones," Sarah suggested.

"I wish," Jack said.

That evening, he called Hope to deliver the unwelcome news.

"I was really looking forward to another chance to see you this weekend," Jack said. "Can you take a rain check?"

"Certainly," Hope said. "Looks like we'll have rain here all weekend anyway."

"I really had fun last weekend," he said.

"So did I. Work hard so you can get back here."

"That's the plan."

He hung up, promising to call her during the weekend.

Six long days later, Jack tiptoed into the room where the weekend team had gathered. No one turned from their monitors to greet him. Pizza boxes spread across the floor, some of them cracked open to reveal grease spots and lonely crusts. Crumpled fast food bags overflowed from the garbage can like a paper-mache volcano. The desks were lined with plastic coffee cups. Pillows still crumpled from the all-nighter on Saturday lay on an empty table. The smell of a college dormitory lingered.

"How are we getting along gang?" Jack asked. "Are we nearly back on track?"

"I think we're doing great," Sarah said, spinning in her chair. The rest of the team kept working.

"So, you're ready to start the testing again?"

"Alex," Sarah called to the corner of the room where Alex was busy finishing his revised code.

"Yeah," he replied, stopping his typing, and removing a pair of headphones. He looked over his shoulder.

"Are we going to get the new code this afternoon?" she asked.

"I already told you once, Sarah. I'll get it to you as soon as I can," he responded curtly.

Someone's chair squeaked, and it seemed to echo in the room. The staccato beat of typing increased awkwardly in tempo.

"I'm sure you'll get it to me, Alex," Sarah replied calmly. "Just let me know if you need any help from my team."

"I will, I will," Alex said. His eyes returned to his monitor.

"When this is all said and done, we're all going to owe you one. We wouldn't be back on track without your magic coding," said Sarah.

"If we ever get done," he muttered, "you can buy me a drink."

"Count on it," Sarah replied.

"You have to admit though, Alex," Jack interjected. "This has to be better than a shark nipping your butt."

"I'm not so sure," Alex responded. He replaced his headphones.

"He's got a point, Jack," Sarah seconded, shrugging one shoulder before returning to her screen.

Jack looked at his watch and realized he still had time to call Hope. He exited the building to see all the Ascend cars neatly parked in the front row. No competition for parking spots on a Sunday.

He called Hope. The phone rang one too many times. His heart skipped a beat.

She finally answered, her voice a bit groggy. "Hello?"

"Hope, this is Jack. How are you?"

"Oh, Jack, so good to hear your voice. I'm sorry, I'm just waking up from a nap."

"How I would love a nap," he sighed, imagining himself nestled up to Hope. Her messy hair draped over him as they lay together on the couch. "Do anything fun this weekend?"

"I just got back from a long bike ride along the Burke-Gilman trail. In the rain. I'm exhausted, but feel good. Did you get to do anything fun?"

"Afraid not. I'm still at the office. Walking around an empty parking lot."

"Oh dear. When are you coming back?"

"I'll be back on Friday," he said. "I'd love to treat you to dinner."

"That would be lovely. Saturday work?"

"Saturday it is. Have you been to Ray's over in Ballard?"

"Yes, I love that place."

"Good. I'll see you then. Bye, Hope"

"Bye, Jack," she said, her voice raspy.

He hung up the phone and stayed walking along the grass medians of the parking lot. He strolled to the edge of the lot to a tiny goldfish pond with two small benches. Sitting down on a bench, he breathed in the cool fall air, waiting for the fish to pass. It briefly surfaced to catch a bug. A small grove of maple trees surrounded the pond. They were now barren, their leaves floating on the pond's surface. Jack thought of the two maple trees next to Hope's apartment. He warmed a bit, took another deep breath, and walked back into the building past the artificial trees, up the winding stairs, through the quiet stale air of an empty office, and burrowed deep into the building, away from the setting sun outside.

The digital tones of his alarm clock woke Jack the following day. He slammed the off button, resigned himself to his fate, performed a creaky push-up, and rose to the morning.

Arriving at the office, he realized he needed his chemical jolt for the day and scanned the conference rooms for Sarah. He pulled her aside and invited her to coffee. They drove to a Starbucks.

Jack walked to the counter and turned to her, "What are you having?"

"I usually like a double-tall mocha, but I love the Ethiopian organic blend and it's the gourmet blend of the month. I'll go with that."

"I guess I'll try that as well." Jack ordered the drinks and paid for them. He turned to Sarah. "So, you actually pay attention to this stuff?"

"Definitely, don't you?"

"Not until recently. I usually just get the regular drip, no questions asked."

"But there's so much more to a cup of coffee. I approach my coffee like wine. Each region has its own unique tastes."

"I'm finding this to be the case. I have a friend in Seattle who practically forced me to go with a gourmet blend."

"Good for her. Did you enjoy it?"

"I guess I must have. I was dreaming about it last night," Jack said. The barista handed them their drinks, and they walked to an empty table and sat down. "How's the testing coming along? I hope we have a good story to tell Ann at the planning meeting this afternoon."

"I think we need until Wednesday to catch up on the schedule. Do you think that will be okay?"

"I don't imagine it being a problem. But it all depends on the client's perceptions. The next bill we're sending them is going to be a shocker. I just need to remind them of the benefits."

"Good luck," Sarah said, adjusting the collar around his coffee. "Sometimes, I pity you trying to work with these guys."

"It can be difficult. But I see how you can calm the personalities on our own team. You've got an art."

"I guess it was the cheerleading in college."

"Maybe. But I have a feeling it doesn't hurt to be a natural leader," Jack said.

"Geez, Jack. I appreciate the comment," Sarah responded.

"No worries. Just keep up the excellent work, and we'll all get out of here with a successful outcome," Jack said. He raised his cup for a cheer. "Let's get back there to rally the troops."

Chapter 8

Jack broke apart a piece of French bread and dipped it into the buttery broth left over from a bowl of Penn Cove mussels, making an S, and forking a couple pieces of garlic onto the bread.

He looked out through the protective plexiglass at an armada of sailboats racing toward the West Point lighthouse. A motorboat plowed its way past a red buoy. Two kayaks knifed through the motorboat's wake and swayed momentarily before gliding toward the Shilshole Marina breakwater.

He turned his attention to his date. Sitting across from him, she grinned, her hair tousled by the wind. Her eyes reflecting the last glimpse of the evening sun. She hadn't broken her glance at the distant Olympics. She wore her brown fleece jacket and her orange beanie. A tan blanket was wrapped tightly around her waist, protecting her from the cool fall breeze.

"What a day," he said. "I mean, you couldn't ask for a better day, even in the summer."

"You're something else right now," Hope said. "You're like a kid in the zoo. I'm expecting you to plaster your face up against the glass here."

"If a seal pops his head up, I just may," he responded.

"You know, your energy level is the complete opposite of our Monday morning visits," she said, sipping an amber ale. She watched as Jack continued to fidget in his chair.

He dipped the other half of the bread into the broth and topped it with garlic. "I guess I'm a different person away from work."

"Definitely a more spirited one," she said. "And one who likes his garlic."

"Yeah, I've got a thing for garlic."

"I love it too," she replied, joining Jack, and dipping a piece of French bread into the broth. "I guess it's the Italian blood."

"That would explain your vigor," he said, "What else is inside those genes of yours."

"I presume you mean genes with a G, right?"

"Ha, maybe."

She picked up her napkin and threatened to throw it across the table. "My dad has the Italian roots. My mom is a mix of Scandinavian. What about you?"

"I've got Celtic blood running in these veins. Mostly Scottish and some Irish," he said. "Have you spent much time in Europe?"

"I've been there a few times, but I prefer to head south. I find staying close to the equator or dipping south to be more raw, untouched than the northern latitudes."

"Yeah, it's funny. I haven't spent much time in that part of the globe."

"You're missing out," she said.

The waiter came to ask for their order. "What is the lady having on this fine evening?"

"I'm going with the salmon."

"And you?" the waiter asked Jack.

"I'll try the seafood linguine."

The waiter left, and they turned to the setting sun. It was dipping behind the Olympics, and the painter in the sky was getting busy with his palette. The sailboats in the distance dropped their sails and floated by the restaurant's deck. Crew members dressed in bright yellows and reds shed their racing gear. Beers were cracked open and passed around on deck. On one boat, a man held a woman closely as they leaned against the mast and watched the colors erupt in the western sky.

"Have you ever gone sailing, Jack?" Hope asked.

"No, but it sure looks like fun."

"It is," Hope said, watching the couple in the sailboat below. She took another drink of her beer. "Do you want to go?"

"What do you mean? Do you have a boat?"

"No," she said with a mischievous grin, "but I think that can be arranged."

"What kind of funny business are we talking about here?"

"Do you trust me?"

"Ahhh... sure," Jack responded.

Darkness had set in by the time they left Ray's. "Are we really going to do this tonight?" Jack asked.

"When else?" Hope replied. "Look at those stars. It's a perfect night for sailing."

"Let's do it then," he said, opening his car door and slipping into his sedan. "I'll follow you." He started his car and watched Hope in the rearview mirror as she skipped down the parking lot, jumping into her green Subaru.

His finger tapped nervously on the leather steering wheel. He recalled a bright summer day years ago at Lake Coeur d'Alene in Idaho. The mad sprint down the wet dock, his impenetrable nine-year-old feet shielding him from the protruding nails. The launch into the water, his legs dangling below him frozen at odd angles. It was so exhilarating and refreshing as he flew from the dock, thrashing through the air. Until he hit the surface and sank below. The crash of the water, submerging below the surface. The gurgling bubbles surrounding him, taunting him. He rose in a panic. The last thing he remembered was the rush of water in his throat and then silence.

And after the silence, there were the panicked voices around him. He opened his eyes, squinting at the midday August sun. The protruding nails of the dock poked his back, the cool sensation of the wet wood on his bony shoulder blades. A shadow of a head drew closer—his sister welcoming him back. From that day on, time in the water, on the water, by the water, would be tainted.

Following Hope's Subaru hatchback down the road, he wondered if there would be lifejackets on the boat. *How far out does she want to go? Will she have a radio in case there's trouble?* He drove closer to her car, squinting to see her bumper sticker. It read ATTITUDE: The difference between ordeal and adventure.

Probably best not to ask, he thought.

When they reached Dock S, he stopped the car. A bottle of wine rolled from underneath his passenger seat. He was glad he bought that for the evening. Reaching over to his glove box, he rifled through CD cases and paperwork and found his trusty Swiss army knife.

She was waiting for him outside his door. "Good thinking," she said, nodding and taking the wine from him. "This will taste wonderful out there."

"I don't have glasses," he said. "I hope you don't mind."

She shook her head. "I can handle it straight from the bottle. In fact, I wish you still had the brown bag. Now, let's get to it."

They walked through the parking lot until they reached a plank that extended down to a row of boats imprisoned behind a tall chain-link fence that guarded the entrance to the dock. Beyond the fence, a forest of masts rose into the night. The sounds of lines clanged against the masts. A seagull stared down from a piling, its head rotating toward them, curious what these two had in mind.

"Do you like to climb?"

"You're kidding, right?"

"Nope, just follow me." She said, attaching herself to the fence. At the top, she turned back to Jack. "You've got to watch out here. There are sharp nails." She carefully straddled the fence and then leaped down to the other side.

He stared at her through the fence. "You're gonna get me in so much trouble." He crouched down to roll the wine underneath the wire and followed her path up and over the fence, sticking his landing with less grace and finesse.

"I have a key, it's just back at my apartment," she said, extending her hand to help him down to the dock. "I promise."

"Sure you do," he said, his head shaking.

She placed her index finger on her lips. "Really, I'll tell you about it in a second."

They walked to the end of the dock. At the last slip, she stopped and pointed to a single-masted fiberglass boat with a green hull. It looked about thirty feet long.

"This is it."

"Are you sure about this?"

"Just trust me," she whispered. "I'm watching this boat for a girlfriend who's out of the country."

"Okay, okay," he said, biting his lower lip and looking down at the ominous black water. He wanted to raise his voice and stop her. He wanted to persevere for her. But he was on the edge. Staring down into an abyss, he froze.

She looked at him while continuing to uncoil the line. "What's up?"

"Nothing," he replied dismissively.

She stopped coiling. "Really? I promise we'll be safe. I can even try to find a life jacket."

He looked up from the dock at her. On the deck of the boat, she was several feet above him. Something about her presence pulled at him. As if the step off the dock and onto the boat's deck was a leap he needed to make.

"Fine," he said, "But you better find a life jacket."

"Great," she said, motioning toward two oars leaning up against a dock locker. "Can you grab those before you step up?"

He picked up the oars and handed them to her. She set them on the left side of the boat.

He stepped onto the boat. It rocked gently. He leaned down and held the lifeline tightly, waiting for the boat to calm down. He shook his head again and bit his lip.

"Now, I need you to hold that tiller there," she told him.

"The what?" he responded, slightly frustrated.

She looked disappointed. "The long wooden stick back there. Can you please grab it and push it all the way to the right side? Then we'll be out of here real soon."

He sat down, comforted by the seat in the cockpit. He shoved the tiller to the right side of the boat. "Alright, got it."

Hope had already untied the boat and was pushing it out of the slip. When the boat's bow had reached the end of the slip, she gave it a big push and jumped aboard.

She ran to the front of the boat and handed him an oar. "Can you go to the port side of the boat and begin rowing?"

"What side is port?" he asked impatiently.

"Sorry, the left side."

Walking gingerly up the side of the boat, he knelt and began to drag the oar through the water. He looked across the boat, and Hope was doing the same on the other side. They glided through the water. When the boat exited the finger of the pier, she hopped back to the cockpit and dropped down into an unlatched storage locker next to Jack. The boat drifted toward the rocky breakwater. Jack was on deck all alone.

"Hope, what the hell are you doing?" His voice trembled. All he could hear was rustling down below. "We're about to hit these frickin' rocks."

"Just a second, just a second," A moment later, she came out with a key and a life jacket. She threw the life jacket to Jack and inserted the key into the engine panel below the tiller. The diesel engine coughed and then chugged itself to life. She grabbed the tiller, corrected the boat's course, and ran a hand through her hair, her face reddened from activity. "And away we go," she said.

Jack remained seated, leaning over the side to see how close they were to the breakwater. "What's next?"

"We haven't even raised the sails yet. That's when it really gets fun." She turned the boat out of the breakwater and into Puget Sound.

A cold, salty breeze hit them square on as they rounded the corner. He looked over at Hope's beanie, wishing he had a hat. He pulled his parka hood over his head and tightened the strings.

Across the Sound, fireflies of house lights fluttered on Bainbridge Island. Menacing whitecaps appeared sporadically on the waves.

Hope asked Jack to take the tiller again. She pointed to the sky. "Just keep the arrow up there on top of the mast pointed straight ahead, and I'll go raise the sail." He followed her command and gripped the tiller.

Hope removed the main sail cover and then looped a line around a winch. She tugged at the line; the sail rose higher and higher with each creak, and when the head of the sail reached the top of the mast, she dropped the line into a cleat. The sail flapped, and the boom swung like an orchestra conductor's hand. She took the tiller again and turned the boat. The sail filled, and the boat heeled to one side.

Jack rearranged himself on the deck as gravity pushed him toward the dark sea. He locked his arms tightly around the lifelines. One slip, and he was in. Every muscle tensed up.

Hope killed the engine. The night became silent. Waves whispered as they tickled the bow of the boat.

"One last thing, just keep our course," she said, handing the tiller to Jack.

She leaned forward and pulled the jib halyard to raise the head sail. Jack tugged on the tiller. The boat heeled even more violently as the full area of the sails swallowed the wind. Waves crashed over the bow. Lines lashed against the mast.

Jack dug his feet into the side of the boat. He was levitating above the water below. He stared at the cold, uncaring water. Visions of a body sinking deeper and deeper into the dark sea flashed before him. The body reached out unsuccessfully for the passing green hull of the boat.

Hope jumped back into the cockpit and took the tiller from Jack, sitting beside him. Her warm thigh rubbed against him. Loosening the main sheet, the sails quieted down, and the boat steadied itself in the evening breeze as she moved the boat downwind. The waves whispered again. She exhaled and smiled at Jack. "So, what do you think?"

"A lot more action than I thought," he said. His knees relaxed as Hope settled beside him.

"I figured you'd like sailing. I just wanted to get out here, kill the motor, raise the sails, and fly through the water."

"So, can we open this yet?" He reached for the wine that Hope had stored in a canvas bag near the cabin.

"We sure can."

Jack opened the bottle and handed it to Hope. "You deserve the first sip."

She took a deep drink. "It's my friend's boat. She's gone to Europe for a year."

"And she trusts you to take it out?" he asked, reaching across for the bottle.

"Why wouldn't she?" she replied with a wry smile. "Now, let me show you how to sail." She handed the tiller back to Jack and leaped around the boat, pointing to tell-tales, cunninghams, boom vangs, and other nautical terms he would soon forget.

When she completed her tour, she sat down beside him with the loose end of a line. "It's time to learn the most important thing of them all: the bowline knot. Just remember the rabbit goes out the hole, around the tree, and back through the hole." She formed the knot several times and handed the line to Jack. He tried a couple of times and failed.

"Don't give up yet," she said, reaching across to grab his hand. "Let me help you."

He let her show him multiple times. Their hands dancing with each other.

"My God, Hope. Your hands are freezing." He rubbed her hands and brought them close to his chest.

"Thanks," she said. "I'd say that's enough instruction for tonight. I am getting cold."

"Just scoot closer here," he said, reaching around and pulling her tight. He felt her ears. "You're really freezing." His arm drew her closer, locking her into place.

Suddenly, the boat bounced off a large wave. Jack's legs tensed below him. He turned toward the dark water.

Hope patted his knee. "Don't worry, Jack. It's nothing." She turned the boat further downwind. The boat quieted again.

He looked across to see the lights of downtown Seattle appear from behind Magnolia Bluff. The only sound was the soft trickle of the boat moving through the water. The honks, the chatter, the fumes of the city so close, yet so far away. Holding Hope closer, his breathing slowed. She was looking forward to the bow of the boat. Her hair spread across his face. He smelled peach shampoo.

The moon rose from behind the Space Needle, and the boat tacked back into the wind. They slowly returned to Shilshole.

The morning sunlight streamed through his condo windows, glinting off the blond streaks in Hope's hair. Wearing one of his Gonzaga sweatshirts and nothing else, she curled up in the corner of his couch, staring out the window.

"Here," he said, offering her a steaming mug before sitting beside her.

She smiled her thanks and took a sip. Her nose wrinkled. "What is this?"

"Coffee."

Shaking her head, she put the mug down on the glass coffee table with a decisive clink. "That, my friend, is not coffee."

Jack laughed, "Sorry, that's all I have here. Tell me what to buy, and I'll make sure I have it on hand next time."

She grinned at him. "I'll pack a pound of freshly ground Tropical."

"Sounds good to me," Jack said. "I can pick some up the next time I'm passing through."

She looked out the window at the water below.

"You were acting strange when we first got on the boat last night? Was something wrong."

He stared down at the dark coffee in the mug. "Yeah, I have to tell you something. I have a terrible fear of water."

She set down her coffee on the side table. "Jack! You should have told me. My God."

"I didn't want to look like a wuss."

"C'mon, Jack. I may be pushy, but I do have empathy. I really wish you would have said something."

"It's alright. I'm really entranced by you, girl. Even if I told you, I still probably would have done it. I find you hard to resist." He grabbed her arm and planted kisses from wrist to shoulder.

She reached over and grabbed her coffee. "How long is this project of yours meant to go on?"

"It should be finished by December," he said. "Why do you ask?"

"I don't know," she said, hugging her mug with two hands. "If we're going to be a thing, it would be good to see you more often."

He squirmed in his seat. "It's only a few weeks longer, let's just see what happens."

Reaching over, he pulled her head to his chest and ran his fingers through her hair.

A plane made its way over the Seattle skyline.

Chapter 9

"Negasi, can you pull over at the Bartell's here?" Jack asked. "I've got some things to pick up."

Negasi turned the car into the drugstore parking lot. Jack had just arrived back in Seattle after being away for two weeks.

Mid-week, he had called Hope, counting the rings.

"Please don't tell me it's another weekend?" she asked.

"I call bearing good news," he said. "I'll be back on Friday. Do you want to come over that evening?"

She hesitated. Jack gulped.

"I'm going to a concert that night," she said.

His heart stopped.

"But I can come over later in the evening?"

He exhaled quietly, holding his hand to his heart. "Great, I'll be ready."

He hung up the phone and looked around the corporate apartment. The blinds were shut, blocking any remaining natural light. The artificial plant in the corner of his living room looked every part dead. A half-eaten sandwich lay on a greasy wrapper, its crumbs strewn across the kitchen table. An empty bag of sour cream and onion chips rested on the wrapper. His coat hung haphazardly on a chair, where he had flung it when he arrived. His computer bag remained closed, the laptop and its responsibilities stored away.

He sank deep into the couch. He was falling into a chasm. A chasm he had visited before. A long-distance relationship. A long-distance relationship made only more painful, more awkward because he was having it with someone from the same city he was supposed to reside in.

He turned his head into his pillow and searched for the scent of her peach shampoo. Closing his eyes , he tried to imagine his fingers tracing the contours of her face. He tried to remember what her laugh sounded like. The way her hair looked uncombed. The way her mouth tasted unbrushed. He was desperate to be home. Desperate to touch.

His pace at work had become more and more robotic. More and more like the computer services he offered Agora, efficient, predictable, and uncaring. He only cared about getting his job done and getting back on the couch to call Hope. He found ways to get out of meetings. At the meetings he did attend, he found ways to keep his answers short like he had something to hide.

He walked into the drug store and headed to the cleaning supplies. He raided the aisle, picking up bleach, scrub brushes, and air fresheners.

He returned to the car and swung two large bags into the backseat.

"Doing some serious cleaning there Jack?" Negasi asked.

"I've got a friend coming over," he said. "And it's been two weeks. That place is going to need a deep clean."

Later that evening, Jack scanned his condo. It looked like it was ready for sale. The granite counters gleamed in the kitchen light. The pillows on the couch fluffed, flexing their mass. A fresh bouquet of flowers sprang from a purple vase.

The buzzer rang, and Jack looked at the video screen. The camera looked down at an orange beanie. Hope looked up and smiled. "You gonna let me in?"

He buzzed her in and reached for a bottle of wine.

The next morning, Jack strolled through the booths at Pike Place Market, his hand locked with Hope's, their arms swinging gently.

They passed a booth of different potted plants.

"Let's stop here," Hope suggested. She spun different pots, grabbing a young poinsettia. "This looks perfect."

"For your apartment?" Jack asked.

"No, for yours," she said, handing the pot to him. "And it needs to be watered weekly. Not bi-weekly. Plan accordingly."

"You are ruthless."

"If you can't handle it, you can always give me the keys to your place."

"Ha, I've seen what you do with borrowed keys."

"Fair point. Let's keep going."

They passed a booth selling Mexican crafts, colorful blankets, jewelry, and papier-mache masks. Hope paused again. She unfolded the blanket and folded it again nicely.

"It reminds me of Guatemala," she said wistfully. "This is similar to the blankets some of the women sewed." She rubbed her hand across the material.

Jack bought the blanket.

They grabbed a coffee at a bakery and zigzagged aimlessly through the market, enjoying their unrushed time together before walking back to the apartment in the early afternoon. The sun had broken through the November clouds, making its way through the condo window and falling on the couch.

Jack unfolded the blanket and spread it over the couch. "Shall we?"

Hope undressed and joined him. They spent the weekend there.

The following Monday, Negasi arrived at the condo. The heavy rain twinkled in his headlights, and the wipers were working overtime to keep the windshield clear.

Hope and Jack exited the condo as the sideways rain lashed the sidewalk. Jack held his coat over Hope's head, his roller back dragging behind him.

Negasi got out of the car and opened the door, and Hope and Jack jumped in. They shook themselves off as they settled into the seat. Negasi returned to the driver's seat.

"Negasi, this is Hope," Jack said. "Hope, this is Negasi. He's been my driver for over a year now. He's as loyal as they come."

"Thank you, sir," Negasi said.

Hope's eyes widened as Jack said, "She's the girl I've been telling you about. She has to work later this morning, so

I figured we could carpool together. Do you mind turning up the heat a bit?"

Negasi reached for the dial and pulled the car onto the street. Jack reached over and grabbed Hope's hand. He shot her a smile and stared out the window. It looked cold outside. It made her hand that much warmer.

Later in the week, Jack's team reached a major milestone. The final software release was ready for production. The team gathered in the Agora executive briefing room, where bottles of champagne chilled in ice buckets. A single desktop machine lay on the table. A group of engineers prepped the team for the final steps while others milled around behind them. Lighthearted chatter filled the room.

Alex sat in the chair in front of the computer. He pecked at the keys, watched the screen, grinned in triumph. He turned to Jack, "Boss, you ready to push the button?"

"Let's do it," Jack responded. "Ready?" His finger hovered over the Enter button. He scanned the room.

"Ready," Alex said, leaning back to give Jack room on his keyboard.

Jack pressed the key and on the screen, a line formed on a graph. It started at zero but soon scaled. "There's our first post-production order."

He pumped a fist in the air. "Congratulations team! We did it!"

Team members pulled the bottles from the ice and passed around flutes. As the team mingled, Ann walked up to Jack.

"I was worried there for a bit," she said.

"That makes two of us," Jack said. He raised his flute to meet hers. "Cheers, it's been fun."

"Your team really impressed me in the end. And it wasn't just me. Agora management noticed as well," she said. "Earlier today, I received an email from the executive team. They want to extend your contract for a second release. You'll be expected to start up again in two weeks."

Jack nearly spit up his champagne.

As the release process wound down, Jack found himself outside the Agora building. It had snowed and a light dusting covered the remaining cars in the parking lot. He started walking toward his car but turned to head toward the pond.

Sitting down on the rock, he dug his hands into his coat pockets and fumbled with the phone, twisting it in his hand. Pressing 4 on the keypad, he found the H and Hope's number. The phone dialed. It started ringing, but he hung up. He wrote a quick text: "sorry, misdialed. Will call later."

He placed the phone back in his warm pocket. The snow started falling again. It drifted down, flakes collecting on the maple branches. Staring up through the trees, he watched his breath drift up into the night air. He exhaled deeply, his lips rattling as snow dropped on his cheeks.

A thin layer of ice had formed on the pond. He wondered how the goldfish would survive the winter, trapped inside, out of options, the frozen surface closing in.

He stood up, unsure of what he would say to Hope. He took a step toward his car, then stopped. Walking to the pond, he reached down to pick up a large rock. Heaving it onto the icy surface, a spiderweb of cracks appeared. He picked up another rock and heaved again. The surface broke, exposing the frigid water.

"Good luck, buddy," he said, returning to his freezing car.

Chapter 10

"Hey, Mom," Jack hollered across the yard. As he stood to wave her over, clumps of sand stuck to his knees crumbled to the ground. "It's already three stories," he said as he pointed to his sandcastle. He wiped his lips dry with his dirty forearm. A five o'clock shadow of sand formed around his mouth.

"Not right now, hon. I'm making dinner," his mom replied from the deck overlooking the sandbox containing Jack. "And you better come inside soon. It looks like it's gonna rain."

"Okay. But first, I want to make one more story," Jack said, twisting and landing with a soft thud. He dragged the plastic cup across the moist sand and used his fingers to compact the sand until it was level with the brim. Examining the pail-shaped third story, he checked for cracks. He covered the cup with his hand and flipped it onto the third story. As the fourth story was set into place, both of his hands backed away in perfect unison as if they were controlled by a master puppeteer. The structure stood, and Jack wiped his lips again in satisfaction.

Only then did he feel the first drop. Like a rain gauge, his palm extended skyward for measurement. Another drop fell again on his shaggy, brown hair. The next landed on his palm and trickled down his forearm. Jack sat, eyes fixed on his castle.

As the drops crashed into his creation, frozen sand puddles formed on each story. The random shape of each puddle kept Jack suspended in fascination. The gentle tap-tap intensified and became something more ominous. The cracks he had meticulously guarded against during construction appeared and grew into destructive fissures. His thoughtful planning was no match for the onslaught of a Pacific Northwest fall evening.

The fourth story was the first to go. Like a house he had seen somewhere after a California quake, the story split violently in two. One more drop sent the remains tumbling down to the third story. The newly formed tears on Jack's face followed a similar trajectory.

Jack shook his head in disbelief. Mom had warned him the rain was coming. But rain is always coming in Seattle, isn't it? His plans to continue after dinner were destroyed. He'd hoped his castle was going to reach six stories. With shattered hopes, he returned to his house.

On his deck, a strange audience assembled. Lined up one by one, he saw his grandfather, his mother, his eighth-grade teacher, his college adviser, and his first girlfriend. They stood shaking their heads in silence. He cocked his arm and hurled his empty cup at them. It missed and bounced several times on the shake roof before rolling down and onto the grass.

"What are you guys doing here?" he screamed. But there were no responses. "I didn't expect it to be like this. I thought it was going to go as planned." Still no response. The group began to shake their heads in perfect unison. "Yes, I'm just as surprised as you. Why do you keep shaking your head?"

"Sir, sir," a deep voice interjected from what sounded like his neighbor's yard. "We're here."

Jack recognized the voice. He tried to make out a figure through the cracks of his neighbor's fence. He couldn't.

"Sir, we're at the airport," the voice continued. A distant honking noise followed.

Jack's eyes opened. The sandcastle ruins, the lineup of family and friends, and the plastic cup in the grass dematerialized into darkness. The symphony of raindrops outside the town car window the only remnant of his dream. He wiped his lips and sat up. He was at Sea-Tac.

"Sorry, Negasi," he said. "I was having one hell of a dream."

"No problem, sir," Negasi replied, getting out of the car, and opening Jack's door.

"Thanks again for coming on short notice," Jack said.

"You're welcome. Kind of strange dropping you here with no bag."

"Yes, I'm on a different mission today," Jack explained. He entered the airport, went to the United ticket counter, and purchased the cheapest one-way ticket he could find to get him through security. His mission objective: Café Escape.

"Jack, what are you doing here?" Hope raised her hands, holding the sky. "Please, please don't tell me you're going to Chicago. You promised me two weeks." Her right hand showed two tall bunny ears.

"Not going to Chicago," he said, shaking his head vehemently. "Do you still have that passport?"

"Of course." She drew the passport from her pocket and displayed it like a soccer referee with a red card.

"And it's not expired?"

"Not expired."

"And you said this Tropical comes from the place where a new dawn has arrived?"

"Yes, Jack."

"And you said you want to go back again?" Jack continued, his speech growing more rapid.

"Yes, Jack."

"To work and help them rebuild?"

"Yes, Jack," she said, her hand rotating to pull more from him. "Where the heck are you going with this?"

"The question shouldn't be where am I going with this. But where are we going with this." He smiled. He felt lighter as the words reached her.

"Have you gone crazy?"

"Probably," he said, his shoulders hunching. "But too late now. I just put in my two weeks' notice. Are you coming or not?"

"Okay. Calm down, Jack. First things first. When?"

"Two weeks. Possibly earlier."

"What about your job?"

"I've already thought about that," he said. "I've got people who can fill in just fine for me. That's how the business world works. Someone's always there to replace you either by choice or by force. I told you about Sarah. The go-getter. She's just got promoted and can take the reins."

"But how are we going to pay for it? I certainly can't afford it right now."

"The tickets are the easy part. I've got enough frequent flier miles to fly this whole café down there. I've already arranged to rent out my condo, and my bank account has some room to flex. At this point, I'm just waiting for you to say yes."

For what seemed like the first time, she paused. She stared at the cash in her hand, looked down at her feet, scanned the faces of her customers. "Of course, yes. Yes. Yes, Yes."

She tore off her apron and walked to the backroom of the café. A few seconds later, she walked out, hugged her coworkers, and then dashed to Jack, planting a wet kiss on his lips. "You really have surprised me, young man. Let's do this."

He showed her the boarding pass for his flight to Bellingham. He tore up the pass. "I won't be needing this one. Let's go to the ticket counter and pick a date."

He grabbed her hand. She followed.

PART II

Chapter 11

As the plane reached cruising altitude and leveled out, Jack peered over Hope's shoulder. The evergreens of the Pacific Northwest faded into the sandy hues of the western deserts. The cabin lights dimmed, and TVs dropped from the ceiling. The flight attendant announced the in-flight movie. Hope placed a set of headphones on and reclined her chair.

Jack switched on the overhead light. He reached into the seat pocket in front of him and opened the airline magazine. He flipped past credit card advertisements and a catalog of useless gifts and stopped at the world map. Guatemala was sandwiched between Mexico, Belize, Honduras, El Salvador, the Pacific, and the Caribbean. He pulled a pen from his shirt pocket and circled the country in thought.

When Hope first revealed the birthplace of his Tropical, he tried to pinpoint Guatemala in his head. He ventured south from the massive swaths of North America into a set of Lilliputian nations squeezed on a land bridge. A bridge whose hold on North America and South America looked brittle. He did not know quite where to place Guatemala. Was it near Panama, where the acne-riddled face of Manual Noriega was indelibly engraved in his head? Or near someplace equally ominous like Nicaragua with its montage of Oliver North, Ayatollah Khomeini, and gun-toting Contras emerging from a thick jungle? Or was it near the tropical paradises where his most adventurous friends vacationed? The white sand beaches of Costa Rica or the turquoise waters that beckoned scuba divers to Belize. During high school, when nightly newscasts accused Central American nations of allowing communism to creep northward, somehow Guatemala escaped the verdict.

The captain interrupted the movie to welcome passengers while playing tour guide to the window seat passengers.

Hope lifted her headphones from one ear. "This captain sure likes to talk. Especially during the good parts."

"I always figured they must have boring co-pilots," Jack said.

She set her headphones on her lap. "I'll have to catch this movie on video."

"I'm happy to tell you how it ends. I've seen it a dozen times already."

"Another perk of frequent flying, I guess?"

"A perk?" He grimaced. "It was like groundhog's day. I'm ready for something different."

She reached over and tapped his circle of Guatemala. "This place should do it."

"Help me get ready. Feed me some details."

"What do you want to know? I'm by no means an expert."

"Oh, great! You know how much I just love surprises."

"Won't it be great though," Hope replied, rubbing her hands together. "Am I going to have to call the flight attendant? Maybe a round of drinks will loosen you up?"

Jack waved down a flight attendant. He ordered a beer. Hope ordered rum and Coke. She shook her cup, making the ice crash around. She took a deep sip. "Let me see, where to begin, where to begin?"

"You can start anywhere because there's not much here," he said, pointing to his head.

"It's a world of contrasts. To me, Guatemala is a perfect example of a terrible beauty. On the one hand, it hosts stunning mountains, magical forests, and ancient Mayan ruins. Yet, lurking in its corners is a terrifying, violent past. A past whose wrath victimized the people for decades. With the Peace Accords, that past, like a defeated dragon, has retreated to its cave. Out of sight, but not out of mind."

"Getting poetic again, are you?"

"Something wrong with that?"

"Not at all. Your enthusiasm is what sold me on this whole idea anyway. Your passion can be contagious, you know."

She placed her hand on his thigh. "I've been told that before. But I've also been told I can be a little *too* passionate."

"I need all of the passion I can get, so keep squeezing." He said, reaching down and tickling the back of Hope's hand.

"Hey, watch it there, I can be ticklish." She launched a short jab on his arm.

"Seriously though," he continued, "I can't wait to see this place with my own two eyes. I just wonder how long this crazy dream will last before I wake and realize what I have done."

"Look at it this way," she said. "Would you rather live a life of dreams or dream of living a life?"

"The former. Or is it the latter? I always get them mixed up."

"While you figure it out, I'm going to enjoy the rest of this movie," Hope said, putting the headphones back on.

Jack flipped back to the front page of the magazine, searching for an article that was worth his time. Unsuccessful, he leaned his head back, closed his eyes, and tried to drift to sleep, wondering where this journey was leading him.

"That coffee was terrible," Hope said as they left the air-conditioned lobby of the Westin Hotel in Guatemala City the following day. Outside, they sat on a bench below a water mister keeping them cool in the early morning sun. "I mean, at least a luxury chain could offer some decent coffee."

"You're probably right," Jack responded, cupping the spray from the mister. "But any coffee is better than no coffee for me."

"I don't know. I was thinking about passing on the cup and just drinking OJ," she said. "And, by the way, I didn't want to ask last night because you were so insistent, but why did you want to stay at the Westin anyway?"

"When you fell asleep after the movie, I pulled out the guidebook I bought at Sea-Tac."

"And?"

"Do you know they have split the city into fifteen zones here?"

"What's so strange about that?"

"Well, when I combined the city's crime rate and the miles of slums, I felt like I was going into a war zone. Zones feel like they are reserved for generals, not tourists. When I heard there was a Westin in Zone 10, a safe zone, I figured it was time to use my reward points. I wasn't ready to meet Guatemala in the dark."

Hope's lips sputtered in feigned disappointment. "Oh, Jack, you kill me. You really do," She raised her hand to flag a taxi.

"And, plus, I always like to start my trips abroad in a nice hotel. That way, I can get a good night's rest after a long flight. Like hunting down a McDonald's in Europe when you feel like greasy American food."

"I understand. I've broken down before too. I didn't get a burger though, I just got french fries. Just as bad, huh?"

"Yes, I'm sure there's an organic potato farmer someplace in Idaho who would let you have it for eating a corporate french fry."

"Okay, okay, I'm begging for forgiveness. Will you grant it?" She fluttered her eyelashes.

"Forgiveness granted. Now, where are we heading?" Jack asked as a white Toyota Corolla with a small yellow taxi sign on its roof swerved around the leafy, half-circle driveway and stopped in front of them.

"We are heading to Zone 1," Hope replied, "we'll catch a bus for Antigua there."

"Zone 1," Jack said, "Let me look that up."

Hope extended her arm across Jack. "No, you don't. Now jump in. I'll put the bags in the back."

Exiting the driveway, they drove along Avenida La Reforma, passing statues of colonial figures guarding the road from their perch in the median strip. At the US Embassy, a huddled mass of Guatemalans crowded under the American flag at the entrance. A tall, imposing gate defended the bright, fresh paint of the embassy. Atop the gate, white security cameras stared down at the crumbling sidewalks where a group of Guatemalans snaked around the corner. Their mottled sea of faded, discolored clothing contrasted with the fresh uniforms of the security personnel standing at the entrance.

Hope and Jack continued down the road, past the Olympic Stadium and into Zone 1. Narrow streets crowded by dilapidated buildings replaced the wide, engineered, palm-lined avenues of Zone 10. The taxi pulled over on the crowded street.

Jack exited the taxi, taking a large step over a pile of empty Coke bottles and a mound of empty potato chip bags. A toothless panhandler swarmed him. Hope deftly grabbed a coin from her pocket and handed it to the panhandler.

Sweat started to seep from Jack's temple as he tightened the grip on his luggage. "Is this the romanticism you were talking about?"

"Kind of. Its rawness is a nice shock."

"Raw is right," Jack said, "And suffocating?"

She pancaked herself and split a passing couple in two. "Or refreshing. Depends on how you look at it. You'll get a hang of it."

He sucked in his gut to let the couple pass. "We'll see."

"And, by the way. Keep your hands at your side. Pickpockets are everywhere. Follow me through these stalls up ahead."

She pointed to a long row of wooden stalls placed directly on the streets. The stalls stretched blocks ahead. Cars zoomed inches away from the stalls, no thought to the throngs of pedestrians. Many of the stalls were constructed and held in place by tattered blue tarps and a jumble of sticks. One stall offered combs, brushes, and toothpaste. The next offered used T-shirts. And the next offered cages of clucking chickens singing their last tunes. Competition was stiff. The inventory of adjoining stalls looked identical. The only contrast was the hawking skills of the vendors. Customers walked back and forth between shops, negotiating for the best deal. A deal created a well-worn path between the shops.

"My God," Jack said. "Where exactly is this bus station?"

"I think I still remember where it is." She waved for Jack to follow.

"You better be kidding," Jack yelled as she maneuvered ahead of him. He followed the blond top of her head as the crowd swallowed her. Feeling the breeze of passing cars on his legs, he realized it was wise to stay close and personal with the stalls.

They continued down three more blocks, and the market stalls became sparser. Clouds of diesel, wafts of cooked maize, a cacophony of voices, and a frustrated jigsaw puzzle of buses marked the bus station. The buses were all former Blue Bird school buses. Yet, none of them were yellow. Each bus repainted with different wild blurs of primary colors. After years of service to the Protestant work ethic in North America, these buses were reincarnated to express their true, artistic selves. Luggage spilled across the roofs, held somehow by the black metal roof racks.

From atop buses, several young men swooped down onto Jack. They crowded around him, screaming destinations.

Jack turned to Hope. "Where are we going again?"

"Antigua," she replied, turning to face the onslaught. A conductor wearing a grease-stained, emerald green soccer jersey grabbed her forearm and pointed to a bus painted like a parrot in bright red and green. The other conductors disbursed like disappointed vultures in search of the next passenger. Hope and Jack followed him.

"My God. They should send Wall Street traders down here. I've never been swarmed like that before," Jack said, using his shirt sleeve to wipe the sweat from his temples.

"Don't worry, I know the feeling. When I first came down here, I was so panicked, I jumped onto the wrong bus and nearly ended up on the wrong side of the country. Pretty exciting, huh?"

"Yeah, real exciting," Jack said, rolling his eyes. "We're actually going to ride one of these?"

"I love these chicken buses. Follow me."

Hope stepped up onto the bus. Jack was close behind.

The driver, a middle-aged man with a well-trimmed mustache and thick, dark wire-rimmed shades, sat resting his forearms on the top of the steering wheel. He looked like an undercover Tijuana detective from a Hollywood movie. He belonged behind the wheel of a souped-up Chevy Malibu, not a reincarnated Blue Bird school bus.

Above the driver's head, worn stickers of Speedy Gonzalez, the Road Runner, and Wiley Coyote stretched across one interior wall. A statue of Jesus stood on the dashboard, its arms stretched to the back of the bus, blessing every row. Hanging from the rearview mirror was a crucifix. Above the crucifix was a certification plate from the Blue Bird Bus Company in Fort Valley, Georgia—a gravestone of the bus's former life.

Jack turned to the back of the bus, expecting to see the green vinyl seats of yesteryear. They were still there but the occupancy ratio was a bit different from what he remembered in elementary school. Instead of two to a seat, the rows were packed with three to a seat and sometimes four when you counted the babies or the chickens. They were all staring at Jack.

"Looks like we're going to have to use the luggage rack outside," Hope said, interrupting his thoughts. She raised her head to the racks above the seats which overflowed with bags, boxes, crates, and caged chickens.

"Sure," Jack replied, "and maybe we can find a taxi or a real bus back out there."

"No way," Hope said. "This is all part of the adventure. Now get out there and help me." She tapped his butt and pushed him out of the bus.

Outside, they handed their bags to the conductor. Springing into action, the conductor ran to the back of the bus and leaped spider-like to the attached ladder—bags in one hand—and scaled the ladder. Dropping the bags on the roof, he ran a rope through them and tied a knot, giving the rope a hard tug. Hope and Jack returned to find a seat.

"Do we get a claim ticket?" Jack grinned.

"Don't hold your breath. But I'm glad to hear your sense of humor is still there. Let's go find a seat. It looks like the driver is ready to go."

Once inside, they found the last seats available near the back. They sat beside an old, leather-faced farmer wearing a straw cowboy hat. The man was deep asleep with his head plastered against the window. Hope sidled next to the man, and Jack joined her, his right leg stretched into the aisle. Balancing on one cheek, he received his first taste of economy-class seating in Guatemala. He looked to Hope, who grinned and looked ahead. The bus revved its engine and maneuvered in fits and starts until it exited the bus station. Jack looked to the crucifix on the rearview mirror and made a small prayer.

The back door of the bus flew open as the bus rolled out of the market, and the conductor contorted his body to wrap around the door and into the bus. The driver accelerated through the narrow streets, oblivious to wandering Hopes and Jacks in the market stalls below.

The conductor stretched himself into harmful-looking positions, squeezed past the passengers, and made his way up the crowded bus, collecting fares as he went. In the front of the bus, he flipped his earnings like a bookie, eyeing the bills. His green jersey seeped with sweat.

Leaving Guatemala City was an ascent to a psychologically different place. Peeking over the lopsided cowboy hat of their seatmate, Jack peered into the distance. Volcanoes rose above the city. Their perfect conical shape made them seem more manufactured than natural. One of the volcanoes was exhaling its breath into the atmosphere. Around its smoking summit, blue hills kneeled obediently to their angry master.

"This is impressive," Jack remarked.

Hope said, giving Jack a golf clap, "I love your enthusiasm."

"Are we heading toward that smoking volcano?" Jack asked.

"No, not that one. But, once you get into the highlands, you'll realize that you can't go anywhere without being a stone's throw away from some volcano. They're like tortillas, they're everywhere."

"That's fine. As long as one doesn't erupt."

"You can never tell, the earth is so active down here," Hope said, "That's what I mean about this place. So beautiful yet dangerous on so many levels."

"I'm getting to see what you mean. Although that crazy market scene had me thinking more terrible than beauty."

After an hour-long ride through the outskirts of the city, up into the hills, and through scattered groves of pine trees, the bus reached Antigua.

The bus stopped in a dusty field, and they stepped off. Jack was amazed to see another set of volcanoes surrounding the town. Hope was right, they are everywhere, he thought to himself. Bell towers poked out above rooftops. A large cross on a nearby hill overlooked it all.

As they entered the city along cobblestones to the central plaza, a moving collage of vivid colors materialized from Indigenous Mayans lining the streets. The women wore richly designed blouses embroidered with multicolored flowers, leopards, or eagles. Colored hair ribbons wove through their waist-length black hair.

Jack passed a baby boy wrapped snugly around his mother's shoulder. His clear, angelic white eyes and raven-black pupils peered innocently out into the mountain's fresh light. When Jack walked past and saw the mother's face, reality reappeared. Her front teeth were missing, and a lesion bled slightly from near her left ear.

They zigzagged at a palm-strewn central plaza filled with young students, resting locals, and groups of tired Mayan children begging passersby for a quetzal. Across the street from the plaza, Hope suggested they stop at a café where patrons were enjoying the cool environs of a lush breezeway of a former Spanish mansion. The mansion opened to a serene garden patio. Hope motioned toward a table near a small stone fountain.

Sitting down on the wrought iron chairs, they exhaled deeply. Palm leaves caught the sun's beams, forming a patchwork of shade. It felt several degrees cooler.

"Oh, does this feel good. I feel like we've been on the move all morning," Jack said, extending his arms above his head. He listened to the tap tap of the fountain over his left shoulder. He thought of the Pacific Northwest. "That fountain reminds me of our first date."

"Oh, that was a date?"

"Whatever you call it, it was the beginning of this." He spread his arms.

Hope looked up from the ground and smiled.

A waiter arrived, and they ordered two cups of coffee.

"I mean, just think about it. Only a few months ago, you enticed me with the charms of this coffee and its magical birthplace. Now, we're here."

"So, what do you think so far?"

"It is something else. The landscape is not what I expected. And I see what you mean about the poverty. Did you see that women's open lesion back there?" Jack asked.

"I did. It's sad. Really sad." Hope looked down to the ground, rolling a pebble with her shoe. "Did you notice the dress she was wearing? It's called a traje. Each village has its own patterns. Some say it was a way for the government to track them."

"Where's our village from here?" Jack asked.

"It's just one more bus stop away," Hope said.

A waiter came and placed two cups of coffee on their table. Jack took the first sip.

"Just like home," Jack said. "A bit sweeter, but the same full body and aroma."

"Very good, Jack," Hope replied. "Despite Guatemala's small size, it holds multiple different microclimates. Each one creates a distinct coffee blend. The Antigua blend is known for its sweetness. The Atitlan blend where we are going is more acidic.

"Atitlan? Isn't that the place *these guys* are talking about going to?" Jack whispered, tilting his head toward the direction of a dreadlocked American couple wearing matching Birkenstocks.

"Good ears. You are correct. Didn't I tell you this plantation owns the finest coffee shop on the shores of Lago Atitlan? I am going to make you a barista yet."

"What?"

"Down boy, down. The coffee finca is in the hills surrounding the lake. It is far removed from the tourist villages. They promised me a warm welcome if I ever returned. I wonder if they ever thought I would take them up on the offer."

Later that afternoon, the bus shifted to a lower gear and began a winding descent to the edge of Lago Atitlan. Jack caught his first glimpse of the ninety-two square mile lake formed thousands of years ago when the subterranean chambers of a massive volcano collapsed, forming a caldera that filled with water. The lake's heavenly shine blinded Jack. The afternoon sun caught the rippled water below, and sparkling dancers pirouetted on the surface. The dancers were surprisingly vibrant, considering the massive, threatening audience of the menacing volcanoes nearby. Like a restless audience ready to jump the stage at a moment's notice, these ominous peaks crowded up against the lake.

The bus stopped at the village of Panajachel. The dreamy view of the lake was replaced with the kitschy aura of a town done in by the tourist trade. In the lakeside market, the stalls of foodstuffs and random accessories were gone, replaced with tables stacked high with colorful handicrafts for the vagabond traveler.

Jack meandered down the street, gasping at the tourist hordes snapping up endless piles of hairpieces, T-shirts, patterned pants, and red, yellow, and green hacky sacks. Hope guided him to a small alley away from the pleading of shopkeepers.

In the alley, they ran into a young, barefooted boy. The boy was standing in a clump of grass on the side of the alley. He pulled out his little one and began to pee. He continued to pee away gleefully, turning his head toward them as if they were in a urinal at the local bar. He smiled and asked if they needed a room to stay in for the night.

"No thanks, senor," Hope swiftly responded.

"A dedicated salesman never stops selling." Jack chuckled.

"Definitely. You won't see a more unique sales pitch than that one."

When they reached the lakeshore, the wind picked up its pace, and white caps formed—no sign of the graceful dancers Jack had seen earlier. He stopped suddenly before stepping into a bouncing wooden boat. "You know I hate the water," he said, his palms breaking into a sweat. "Is this the only way to get there?"

"It's the fastest," Hope said. "We did this in Seattle, we can do it here. Jump on in."

He stepped in and grabbed the gunwale, sitting on the middle seat of the boat. Hope followed. A man wearing a backward New York Yankees hat expertly pulled the start cord, and the engine hummed to life.

As the boat pulled out from the dock, Hope placed her hand on Jack's thigh. "I've seen that look before."

"Yeah, yeah," Jack said, looking forward and inspecting the driver's path through the whitecaps. He nodded. "God, I hate this."

The boat took a large wave and splashed into the water. Jack gripped the gunwale tighter. He closed his eyes and tried to keep the contents of his stomach in place.

A bumpy, wet ride later the lancha reached a small bay. The rising land quieted the waters. Jack exhaled as the boatman cut the engine and expertly turned the boat into a rickety, wooden pier that poked out from the reedy shoreline. The pier yielded, ever so slightly, and the boatman leaped to the pier, holding the bow in place.

Jack stepped off the boat, careful not to slip through one of the patchy wooden planks. He extended a wet palm to Hope, clasped her hand, and pulled her up. The boatman passed their bags to them, and they turned to walk off the pier, to where a set of buildings stood in a grove of pine trees.

Outside a small restaurant, they jumped into another of Guatemala's transportation oddities—a Toyota pickup converted into a people carrier. A metal frame covered the camionetta's bed. Passengers crowded into the back. They stared at Hope and Jack, who grabbed the metal cage and swung into the back. They slid their bags to the front of the bed next to a pile of corn and watermelon.

"Can you imagine what would happen if this truck had to stop suddenly?" Jack asked, balancing himself.

"No, I wouldn't want to imagine. Nor should you," Hope replied as the camionetta got underway, and her hair galloped in the wind.

"This heat is something else," Jack said.

"We'll have to come down to the lake to refresh ourselves. Maybe even a swimming lesson or two, huh Jack?"

"Maybe," he said, looking up at the mountain away from the water.

Winding its way up the mountain, the road got steeper and the sun hotter. Off to the side, piles of wood were randomly set on the road, and soaked men, women, and children were standing by them, sweat cascading off their faces.

"They go into the forest here to pick up wood for their fires because most of these people have no electricity," Hope explained.

A father and his son appeared, carrying a load of sticks wrapped around their bodies. This was not just an ordinary-size load. These loads were the size of the carriers. Driving up behind them, it looked like a walking pile of wood with dirt-covered human feet—something only Tolkien could dream up.

The next winding corner brought another surprise. On the side of the road, leaning forward and straining with all his might, was a middle-aged man pushing his ice cream cart up the side of a volcano.

The camionetta stopped where a narrow dirt road full of deep ruts led into the pine forest. The driver yelled, "Nuevo Amanecer" and Hope and Jack slimmed themselves to get past their fellow passengers and stepped down from the pickup, ducking their heads to avoid hitting the metal bar.

"We're here," Hope said, dropping the bags on the ground.

As the camionetta sped away up the hill, a cloud of dust billowed around them.

Chapter 12

When the dust settled, Jack was surprised to find an elderly woman standing next to him. She was dressed in an ankle-length black skirt and wore an azure blouse embroidered with a sold, royal blue ribbon across the chest. Dirt blanketed her sandaled feet. She held a large red plastic tub full of something that looked like corn flour. Her face held an endless maze of wrinkles, and her raven black hair, worn in a single braid that reached below her shoulder blades, was beginning to lose the war against an invading gray army of age. Tucked in between the wrinkles, two sparkling orbs hovered brightly, rejecting any attempt by old age to wither them.

With the surprise rendering him speechless, the elderly woman spoke first.

"Where are you young travelers going?" she asked. Jack turned to Hope. He could make out the Spanish but hesitated to answer.

"We're headed to Nuevo Amanecer," Hope replied.

The woman's eyes widened.

"Do you know of it?" Hope asked.

"Of course, my son is the director."

"And what is his name?"

"His name is Pedro."

"Pedro Castilla?"

"Yes," the woman said, pausing, scanning Hope from head to toe.

Hope placed her hand on her heart and smiled. "He is the director now. That's wonderful."

"And how do you know my son?"

"I lived and worked here three years ago."

"Is your name Hope?"

"Yes, it is."

The woman smiled broadly, revealing two gold teeth that shone in the afternoon sun. "It is so great to meet you." She reached out both hands. She held Hope's hands in place, shaking them gently. "Pedro has told me wonderful things about you. I am sure he will be so happy to see you."

"And I can't wait to see him. Is Pedro around? We would love to talk with him."

"Unfortunately, Pedro is in Guatemala City trying to find a new exporter. The prices are the lowest they have been in years. Times are tough, I'm afraid." Her wrinkles seemed to multiply.

Jack interrupted, trying to interpret the look of consternation. "What was she saying about the coffee price?"

"Coffee prices are at an all-time low. I was worried about that back in Seattle. It's been putting a lot of pressure on production everywhere, and it sounds like they have not been spared here," Hope said, turning back to the elderly woman. "I do recall Pedro's stories about you, but I remember he said you were still in Chiapas. When did you return?"

"I returned three months ago after my husband passed away."

"Oh, I am so sorry to hear that."

"It is okay." She lifted both hands toward the sky. "Life and death are part of the same cycle. My ancestors would say he is ascending the roots of the great ceiba tree to ride the branches upward to heaven."

"Jack, are you getting this?" Hope asked, her eyebrows raised.

He nodded. "Bits and pieces. But keep going."

Hope turned back to the elderly woman. "I'm awfully sorry, but can you remind me of your name?"

"Certainly, it is Isabella."

"Nice to meet you Isabella, and welcome home."

Hope placed her hand gently on Jack's forearm. "This is my friend Jack."

Isabella extended her hand to Jack. "Pleasure to meet you, Jack,"

"It's a pleasure meeting you, Isabella. I look forward to meeting your son Pedro as well," Jack said in sputtering Spanish.

"You are both very welcome here."

"Thank you," Hope said. "If Pedro is not around. I hope we'll find Maria."

"Of course, let us go," Isabella said, grabbing the tub with two hands, raising it, and setting it softly on her head.

"Can I help you with that?" Jack asked.

"Of course not. I will be quite alright." She turned and began to walk down the road, the tub perfectly balanced on her head.

Jack and Hope followed. "Oh, lovely Maria, I miss her so much," Hope said. "I remember waking each morning to the sight of Maria's backside tending to the morning fire. She would twist her head, and her long braid would always seem to flop the same way onto her right shoulder. She would wish me a good morning and ask if I wanted a coffee before my morning walk. I can't wait to see her."

They hiked for about half a mile until the road forked. Isabella pointed to the left, and the road started to descend toward the distant lake. Behind them, the hill rose steeply, and Jack could make out the cloud-shrouded Volcán San Pedro. The road narrowed, and vegetation covered the centerline. The afternoon sun reflected off the lake, and its intensity grew. Jack could smell the heat with each breath. Sweat began to drip from his neck. Mosquitos soon followed.

He swatted a mosquito away and stepped over the chaparral shrubs creeping onto the road. "Doesn't look like cars get down here very often."

"It was only the occasional truck during harvest season," Hope said.

He looked ahead to Isabella, who was marching ahead, her feet navigating gracefully around the obstacles on the path. "Not a single bead of sweat."

After another half-mile walk, the path turned, and Jack was surprised to see an ornate, black wrought iron gate materialize across the roadway. Behind the gate but blocked from full view by an emerging forest of leafy pines, a handful of red corrugated tin roofs sat quietly. Seeping through the canopy beyond the buildings, smoke rose and dissolved into the blue sky.

Nearing the open gate, Jack noticed an intricate letter H on the left gate and, on the right gate, a letter D. He stopped and pointed at the letters.

"Hermann Diesseldorf," Hope said.

"That doesn't sound very Guatemalan?"

"His family owned the finca for nearly sixty years before they lost the land in the mid-1950s during the agrarian reform."

While they were talking, Isabella had placed her tub on the ground. She walked toward them.

"He was a very rough man," Isabella started. "My grandparents and many of our people suffered under the many Germans who came to Guatemala."

"What happened to them?"

"In the 1950s, we had a government that suddenly cared for us. They treated the workers as equals with the elites. The German plantation owners did not like these policies, some of them returned to Germany, some remained. But our revolution was short-lived."

"Why?" Jack asked.

"Your government came."

Jack placed his hand on his chest. "My government?"

"In 1954, the CIA came and helped overthrow the government. And then we swapped the German plantation owners with our own local elites, and the cycle of tyranny began again." Isabella grabbed the gate and stared at the H. She gently shook it. "It lasted for thirty-six years."

Jack was speechless. Hope looked at him, her eyes saying I told you so.

Isabella walked down the path. She picked up her tub again. "We better get going."

As they passed beyond the gate, the vegetation changed from a mishmash of shrubs to short, emerald trees lined in rows. The trees filled both sides of the road, up and down the ravine. Random scatterings of gray-barked pines towered like sentinels, casting long shadows across the short trees. Red-chested birds soared silently between the pines.

"Coffee?" Jack asked, pointing to the short trees.

Hope reached out to a tree, exposing a branch with a long row of small cherries, some green, some fire red. She picked a red cherry and bit into it. She took out two seeds and a thin layer of pulp. "Yep, these two seeds will be born again as coffee beans. Give this a taste." She handed a piece of the pulp to Jack.

"Sticky. Starts off sweet like a raspberry but ends up tart like a cranberry. How could something so brilliant red turn my teeth so yellow?"

Turning the corner, a massive, whitewashed home appeared. It was nestled on the high side of the road with an expansive view of the lake below. Its white paint was flaking off, and Jack seemed to make out bullet holes in the walls. Green shutters hung precariously from shattered glass windows. Gutters swung in the wind. Broken terra cotta roof tiles lay shattered on the ground below. Hungry wisteria had devoured parts of the home.

As they passed, Isabella turned to Jack and waved her finger. "Casa patronal. It is haunted by the ghosts of the past."

Jack turned to Hope. "Hermann's house, I presume."

"Yes, they won't touch it."

"Would make for a nice B&B."

Hope copied Isabella, who was waving her finger in the air. "Don't even think about it."

Next to the home, two women worked diligently in a well-tended garden.

They looked up as Isabella, Hope, and Jack walked by, their hands still digging into the earth.

"Is this new, Isabella?" Hope asked.

"Yes, the community wants to start a coffee tree nursery. We don't have everything we need right now, but the garden patch is a start. The trees have suffered from years of war. We need to prepare for their replacements. It will take a large investment from the community."

Past the casa patronal, there were warehouses in varying states of disrepair. Unlike the home, these buildings still served a function. Some were padlocked shut. Others hosted mountains of empty burlap sacks whose summits reached the ceiling of the building. Large equipment was in one building, and men were busy with rags cleaning the rusted parts while another man mopped the floor. Jack could smell wet dirt and cement as he passed. The buildings formed three parts of a large square. A flat bare concrete surface surrounded by a three-foot-tall cement wall lay in the middle. The fourth side of the square was open to a long, deep trough that ran along the perimeter of the square.

"The coffee patio," Hope said. "You'll learn all about that."

They followed Isabella along a narrow path that disappeared into a grove of banana trees. In between the stumps, barefooted children were kicking around a torn soccer ball. Three dogs did their best to play along. At the sight of Hope and Jack, the children froze.

"Buenos tardes," Hope said, making a wide wave with both hands. A shocked chorus of high-pitched voices returned her greeting with multiple "Buenos." Jack followed her lead with a "Como esta?" and the chorus unleashed a refrain of giggles.

Leaving the banana trees, they arrived at the homes of Nuevo Amanecer. Lined up along a long, wide path were three rows of homes constructed from concrete blocks. Red corrugated tin served as roofs. Bedsheets functioned as curtains for the glassless windows. Bright 7up and Pepsi posters covered one home. A handheld radio perched on one of its windows. Jack could make out a soccer announcer in between bursts of static. Behind each home was the source of the plumes of smoke he had noticed earlier. Every home hosted an open cooking area where women tended to their fires in the early evening sun. Wafts of cooked chicken and maize permeated the air.

At a nearby fire, a short, stocky woman turned her head when she heard the encroaching footsteps. Her long-braided hair flopped onto her right shoulder.

"Hope?" She squinted, dropping her wooden spoon onto the stone shelf beside her. "Is that you?"

Hope ran toward her with outstretched arms. She gave her a hug.

"It is you, Hope." The woman leaned back to cup Hope's cheeks with both hands. "I am so happy to see you,"

A tear broke down Hope's right cheek, and she settled her head sideways on the top of the woman's head. "Maria, I've missed you so much."

Breaking their embrace, Hope kept one hand on Maria's back. She gestured to Jack with her free hand. "This is my friend Jack."

"Jack, it is a pleasure to meet you," she said.

"It is a pleasure to meet you as well," Jack said.

"I hope you will join us for dinner?" Maria asked. "Carlos and Elizabeth will be very excited to see you."

"Of course," Hope said, grinning at Jack. "We have no plans."

"Great," Maria said. "Isabella, can you help get the table set and let our guests get comfortable? I will go round up another chicken."

Isabella brushed aside a nylon curtain and led Hope and Jack inside. She pointed to a wooden table covered with a rose-patterned plastic tablecloth. The table was centered on a bare dirt floor. Surrounding the table were five metal chairs with brown seat cushions— ubiquitous ones used in every school assembly in the United States. Taking a seat, Jack rested his weary legs. Even the wafer-thin cushions of the seats were a welcome treat.

He scanned the room. On one side were two twin-sized wooden cots covered with faded yellow sheets. A glossy magazine with tattered corners rested on one bed, a soccer player wearing a sky blue and white jersey posed mid-air on the cover. In between the beds was a short, stubby mahogany dresser. A stone propped up one leg of the dresser. A bleeding crucifix overlooked both beds. Against the opposite wall, cardboard boxes were stacked—some overflowing with dangling sleeves and pant legs, others holding aging newspapers. A poster of Che Guevara hung next to a poster that memorialized a deceased, spectacled Bishop named Juan Jose Gerardi on another wall.

"Can I get you a cup of coffee while we wait?" Isabella asked.

"Yes, please," Hope answered.

Isabella left to retrieve hot water from the fire outside. She returned with a white plastic coffee pot. As she poured, the coffee's steam infused into Jack's nose, and his thoughts drifted thousands of miles back to Café Escape.

"Hope, is this what I think it is?" Jack said.

"Well, there's no telling, to be honest," Hope responded. "My manager bought the coffee from an importer of Guatemalan coffee. I never really knew the exact origins."

"Wait, just one moment." He thought back to Hope's dramatic story about the Tropical. "I thought the Tropical came from the land where people are starting over again or something like that."

"I knew it was from the Atitlan region, but I was never entirely sure. A girl can dream, can't she?"

"Yeah, you are good at that." Jack blew softly across the coffee, and its warmth ricocheted back across his upper lip. The nutty aroma followed.

A crescendo of distant voices and bouncing soccer balls echoed off the concrete walls outside. Following a series of "hasta mañanas," a set of footsteps broke out from the rest. Arriving at the doorway were a teenage boy and a younger girl. The boy burst Hulk-like out of a plain white T-shirt, his black jeans speckled with dirt and torn at the left knee. Wearing blue plastic flip-flops, he held a black and white soccer ball under one arm. The girl wore a blue shirt with a daisy pattern and a white-trimmed pink skirt tattered where it reached her ankles. She wore pink flip-flops.

Their youthful energy dissipated into the evening air, and they halted as they entered the room.

"Carlos? Elizabeth?" Hope asked.

The girl ran. The ball dropped out of the boy's hand and bounced away outside the home. He followed. "Hope!" the boy and girl screamed in unison, encircling her with a hug.

"Is it really you?

"It is me. Carlito, Liz, so good to see you. You have both grown so much." Hope said as she held each of them in one arm.

"Do you know I'm studying English and—"

"I'm the captain of our soccer team," Carlos interjected.

"—and geometry," Elizabeth continued, staring down her brother.

"Alright, alright. One at a time," Hope said. "But, first, I want you to meet someone." She introduced Jack, who extended his hand for a handshake. They obliged for a moment before turning back to Hope.

Maria hollered from outside where she was preparing the dinner. "Can you let them rest and go find more chairs?" They hunched their shoulders and left.

Maria entered bearing glass plates holding roasted chicken pieces, white rice, and black beans. She placed a red plastic tortilla holder in the middle of the table. The room seemed to warm in the presence of the food. Jack's stomach churned. The children returned with two faded forest-green plastic chairs, and they all sat.

Maria led the group in a small prayer. As they ate, Maria described the growing pains of Nuevo Amanecer. Despite their best efforts, the women's cooperative was still having difficulty finding markets for their weavings. The coffee market was also not improving. Prices had not increased for months, and competing against the larger, more established fincas was a struggle. Some of the nearby fincas had recently ceased operation. Crime was on the rise again.

Hope and Jack described what they did back home. Jack had a challenging time explaining his old job. He concluded that the easiest explanation was that he was a computer mechanic for large companies. Hope's work at the café was understandable by everyone. It was the end of the line for their coffee beans. When she told them the price for a cup of coffee, color seeped from the faces across the table.

As they were finishing up their dinners, Maria sat back and placed her hands on her lap. "So, what is your plan, Hope? Do you plan to stay again, or are you just passing through this time?" Hope looked to Jack. Jack looked at Hope.

He took a sip of coffee. "We don't have a definite plan. We are trying to take things one cup at a time."

Hope grinned in approval. "Jack's right. We're ready for a recharge, and we're here to help. We'll let fate handle the rest."

Isabella, who was silent during dinner, interjected, "Sometimes it is good to turn to the spirits and let them guide you to new heights."

"Thank you, Isabella," Hope said. "I like that perspective."

Maria smiled, looking fondly at her mother-in-law. "You are welcome to stay as long as you like. Pedro should return tomorrow, and he will have ideas for you both."

She stood and started clearing the plates. "Let me take your dishes, and Carlos and Elizabeth can escort you to the warehouse to find mattresses. For tonight, we will put you two in the corner over there," she said, pointing to the wall where the stack of boxes nearly reached the ceiling.

They followed the children past a group of women scrubbing dishes in a set of tubs and through the banana trees to one of the warehouses surrounding the coffee patio. Carlos slid open a door, and the musty smell of storage overcame the quartet. Carlos entered the warehouse, reached between a snarl of furniture, and pulled out two yellow foam mattresses.

Jack grabbed them both, and they returned to the house. Maria and Isabella were lifting the final box and hauling it into the second room of the house when they returned. Peeking through the drawn curtain, Jack saw a queen size cot with a wool shawl across it and a four-drawer dresser. On the dresser was a sombrero and a short stack of books, one of which looked like a frayed Bible. Returning from the room, Maria held two candles in her right hand.

"We are lucky enough to have electricity, but like many things, it can't be counted on. And today is one of those days," she said, lighting both candles and tipping them to let the wax pour into a pool on the floor.

"You two have had a long day. Why don't you rest your heads and get a good night's sleep?" She set each candle into the pool of wax and disappeared behind the curtain. "Carlos and Elizabeth, can you walk your grandma home and let Hope and Jack get ready for bed?"

Isabella wished them goodnight and left with Carlos and Liz.

Jack set his bag up against the wall and riffled through it, looking for his toothbrush.

"Is the fresh water still in the back?" Hope asked Maria.

"Still there," she said, "The recent rains have helped fill them."

Hope grabbed a candle and walked outside to a large, black water tank. She lifted the lid and placed a plastic jug into the water.

"Here you go. Try not to swallow too much."

Jack brushed, spat into the banana trees, and followed Hope back to the house. Bugs circled the candle's flame, and he could hear them buzzing. His eyes grew heavy from the weight of the day. He was too tired to process any of it.

When they returned, the mattresses were covered with sheets. Two thin pillows rested at the head of the bed. The pillows looked as tired as Jack felt.

He placed his toothbrush back into his bag and slipped into bed. Hope opened a bottle of water and offered Jack a sip. He took a large swig. She blew out the candles, and the smell of wax permeated the room.

He closed his weary eyes. The last thing he heard was the soft footsteps of the children returning and a softer whisper from Hope wishing them good night. He fell fast asleep.

Chapter 13

He woke to a house preparing breakfast. Maria placed a tall stainless steel coffee pot on the table and went back outside to tend the fire. The children's beds were empty. Hope held two bright yellow towels over her forearm.

"You ready for a shower?"

He pivoted, dropped his feet to the floor, and raised his arms to stretch.

"Coffee first?"

"Makes sense," Hope said.

He sorted through his bag, searching for clothes, and sat at the table. Raising the cup to take his first sip, he pointed his chin to the children's bed. "I didn't hear them leave. Where did they run off to?"

"It's a school day. They wake every morning to catch a camionetta up over the ridge to the nearest secondary school."

"How long of a ride is it?"

"I'm not sure." She hollered outside to Maria. "How long does it take for Carlos and Liz to get to school?"

"About one hour."

"One hour on the back of a camionetta. That would wake you up," Jack said, remembering his wet, groggy elementary school bus rides back in Seattle.

"A cold shower will wake you too."

"Cold, huh?"

"Yes, today I will introduce you to a good ole bucket shower."

Jack took one more sip of coffee. "Okay, let's do this."

They left the house and walked through the banana grove. Two tall, narrow outhouses constructed of corrugated metal siding stood between two pines. A set of concrete steps rose to the doors. The building on the left had a large red tub like the one Isabella held on her head the day before. There was a pitcher floating in the tub.

"That one's the shower. The bathroom is on the right. You good?"

"I think so," Jack said. He draped the towel over his neck and entered the building on the right. Sunlight streamed through a crack in the ceiling, providing Jack with just enough light to see that there was no toilet. Just a hole in the floor and a roll of toilet paper sitting on a horizontal two-by-four holding the wall up. A roll with little paper left.

When he exited, Hope was pouring steaming hot water into the red bin.

"I decided to go easy on you." She looked up through a cloud of steam. "You'll have plenty of time to get used to cold ones."

He closed the shower door and dragged the tub into the shower. A small hook on the inside of the door gave him a place to hang his clothes. He inspected each wall for spiders and closed his eyes. The water trickled down his face and he pretended for one moment to be in a hotel someplace back in the US. He opened his eyes just in time to see a large, black and white spider make its way across the ceiling. He finished up quickly and returned to the house.

Hope chatted away with Maria and Isabella like old friends. She was already settled in, it appeared.

"How was it?"

"Great," Jack said with a slight grin.

She punched Jack on the shoulder. "Atta boy." She rose from the table. "My turn."

"You may want to get some more toilet paper," Jack said, raising his eyebrows.

"You betcha."

Jack sat quietly at the table, sipping his coffee, waiting for Hope to return. His mattress from last night was up against the wall. He reached into his bag and pulled out his watch. It read 8:36. He was in the same time zone as Chicago where his team was probably trickling into the office. Maybe Sarah had already stepped up to lead them. He wondered if he was missed.

While he was thousands of miles away, Hope returned from the shower. "That felt wonderful." She shook her head like a dog, and water leaped from her hair onto Jack.

The spray brought him back to reality. "Cold or hot?"

"Cold, of course."

Maria entered from outside, balancing plates on her hands and forearms. She set fried plantains, scrambled eggs, and refried beans in a triangle on the table. Off to the side, she added a small bowl of salsa. "Please help yourself. I'll return with the tortillas in a second."

Jack hesitated to start eating, but Hope's encouragement and her first scoop of eggs were too much. He grabbed his fork, dove into the typical triad of Guatemalan breakfast food, and played around with the combinations of tastes and textures.

When the tortillas arrived, he built a breakfast burrito. Laying a hot tortilla gently on his palm, he briefly enjoyed the heat on his skin. He applied a layer of beans, arranged the eggs on top, and spread a spoonful of salsa before folding the tortilla to complete the job. On his final bite, he experimented with a bit of the fried plantain as well. Not exactly a perfect match, he thought to himself.

Hope ate with two hands fully engaged. "This is the local way," she explained. Using her left hand to hold an empty, rolled tortilla, she used the fork in her right hand to create varying medleys. "The everything-but-the-kitchen-sink with our tortillas back home is an American-born phenomenon," she said.

Jack grabbed another tortilla and bulldozed bits and pieces across his plate to create a final bite. He watched as Maria, Isabella, and Hope conversed over their food.

A man wearing a sombrero suddenly appeared in the doorway. He wore a vertically striped black and white cowboy shirt unbuttoned at the top. Creeks of sweat crept around his neck, making his gold necklace and cross glisten. He wore a belt with a large oval buckle. His gray pants were tight-fitting, and somehow, his black shoes still shone. His hair was the familiar raven black, and his thick mustache covered his upper lip and extended on its lateral edges well past his mouth. A thick scar started above his right eye and continued below his eye onto his cheek.

As he entered, he caught Jack's eye. His forefinger was resting against his lips. This was a man used to walking quietly.

Jack turned robotically to his left. He brought the coffee to his mouth and drowned the remaining tortilla bits.

The predator moved in on his prey. Silently placing one foot in front of the other, he locked eyes with Maria. As with Jack, he indicated his intentions. Maria's eyes returned to her plate.

Crouching down to one side of Hope, the man extended his neck, ostrich-like. "Buenos Dias," he sang into Hope's ear.

Hope turned and smiled—a bit of bean remained stuck between her teeth. She kicked back her chair and hugged him, resting her chin on his shoulder. Jack noticed her using her tongue to dislodge the bean. She blushed and shrugged.

"How have you been Hope?" he asked as they split apart.

"I've been wonderful, Pedro. I am so glad to see you."

"And I you," he said and turned to Jack. "What has brought both of you here?"

"We left the US a couple of days ago. We're taking a break, and we thought we could help." She paused. "That is, if you need…"

"Hope, you don't need to finish. Of course, we would love your help again. And the help of your friend whose name is…"

"Jack," she said.

He extended his hand. "Nice to meet you. We are delighted to have you. My house is your house."

Jack was impressed with his grip. The combination of the firm grip, the calloused skin, and the muscles made it difficult to distinguish where the bone ended and the muscle began. Dirt lined each of his fingernails.

"Are you sure you can take us on?" Hope interrupted.

"No problem. You were so helpful last time. How long are you planning on staying?"

This time, Hope spoke first. "As Jack likes to say, we don't have a plan. It is one cup at a time," she said, reaching for her coffee and grinning at Jack.

"Okay, then, let's figure out a place for the two of you." He chewed on his lower lip, his mustache dancing. "Follow me. I've got the place," he said, waving his hand.

They followed Pedro down to the end of the row of houses. "This house here is empty. Their son got sick, and we couldn't take care of him here. They moved back to Xela."

Jack and Hope entered. The home was empty, the floor bare dirt. "This will be perfect," Hope said. "Right, Jack?"

"Right," Jack responded, looking around the inside of the empty home.

"I'll have someone bring the mattresses, and we'll get some cots built. We'll have you at home in no time."

"And, Pedro, one last thing. Along with our time, we'd like to give something back to the community."

"Not now, Hope. I trust you will. For now, you just settle in."

Later that evening, Hope and Jack lay on mattresses atop a straw mat over the dirt floor. Apart from their two bags, the space was sparse. Jack could smell the sweating concrete blocks of the wall and the wet earth next to him.

"I don't know Hope. Maybe we should just stay a few days, make a donation, and then head back to Antigua. This may be pushing my limits."

"Jack, c'mon. You'll get used to it. Pedro says we'll have a cot tomorrow, and we can head to Xela to get some bins for clothes. We'll make it our home."

"I don't know. I don't know."

Hope reached over. Her arm rested across his chest. She whispered into his ear, "At least we have some privacy."

Jack looked at the flimsy curtain door fluttering in the wind. He wasn't so sure.

Chapter 14

"Where have you been?" Jack asked, using his finger to dislodge the gunk stuck from his eyes.

"I've been out for a walk." Hope took a deep breath and wiped her forehead with a red bandanna. "I like to get out and stroll the countryside in the mornings before the heat tries to bake the energy out of me." She explained that morning walks were her chance to sort out and prepare for the day, when the world was a quiet, innocent place. A place where birds sang, morning dew lingered after it washed the earth, and the sun's rays woke the world. It was at this time that she entered her garden, ready for battle, looking for the wrongs of the world. Alone. Breathing the crisp, moist air. Finding a path to contentment.

"You mean there is a way to quell your energy?"

"Maybe not quell it, but certainly redirect it. Have I ever told you the story of the elderly woman I followed once in the Japanese garden at the Washington Arboretum?"

"You haven't."

"She's my inspiration. One winter day, I was following this squatty gray-haired Chinese woman. She was wearing dark blue silk trousers with bamboo imprints and a white blouse. Her hands were locked behind her back. She barely kept up with the snails in the grass beside her. She had this aura about her. It was as if she was glowing. Glowing as she arranged and rearranged the jigsaw puzzle of life. I try to do the same on my morning walks. I may not have the puzzle finished, but I'm making progress. I try not to let the challenges stop me. Eventually the puzzle will be finished." She shrugged.

"So where do you go?"

"I've got a whole bunch of routes. I tried to do this every morning the last time I was here. I'm going to start the tradition again. Maybe I can get you out of bed one of these days to come with me."

"Maybe," Jack said, knowing the chances were slim. Mornings were not the optimum time for him to partake in exercise. His joints were glued together, his mind was scattered, and his stomach was empty. He'd tried jogging with the morning people at work. Those early birds could wake, skip breakfast, and somehow bring their heart rate to fever pitch before a shower and the rest of the world was awake. They had a strange affinity to the rising sun—no vampires were in that group.

When Jack tried the morning run, he would return with a momentary adrenaline rush, and for a brief second, he thought he would do it again. By mid-morning, he had his doubts. He found himself exhausted, and whether it was re-reading the same sentence several times or re-writing the same email several ways, his productivity dwindled. If he substituted a morning workout for a shower, a coffee and breakfast, he was fine. His time for exercise was in the afternoon, if at all.

"Have you eaten yet?" Jack asked, rubbing his stomach. "I'm starving."

"I haven't, but I passed Maria's home and she's got a pot of coffee and some breakfast ready for us. Pedro will be here shortly to show you around."

They walked back to Maria's where she'd placed two chairs outside in the morning sun. She handed them each a plate. Jack thanked her profusely and dug into his food. Isabella appeared from inside the house with two cups of coffee.

Pedro walked in as they finished breakfast. "Are you ready Jack? I want to give you a quick tour, and then we'll get you into the ravine."

Jack turned to Hope. "What about you?"

"I'm going to Panajachel with Maria. I'd like to pick up some stuff for our place. Pedro will look after you."

"Okay, fine," he said, carrying his plate to Maria. He offered to help her clean the dishes, but she shooed him away with her hand.

Hope's eyes tracked him as he walked past. "You okay, Jack?"

"I'm good," he said. "I just realized this will be the first time I have you out of my sights."

Hope walked over to give him a hug. "Here's to new adventures." Resting his chin on her shoulder, he held her close for a moment longer and tilted his head back to look into her olive eyes. They were sparkling, and he wondered what his eyes were doing.

Jack tried to keep track as Pedro led him through the row of houses, proudly naming them by the family who occupied them. As they wandered past neighbors, he was quick to introduce Jack. The smallest children hid behind adult legs, giggling. A group of older children chased a pack of emaciated dogs through the banana trees, threatening them with a fallen banana leaf.

They walked in the direction of the front gate, and when they reached the warehouses, they turned left and went deeper into the ravine. Down a small, winding path, they arrived at two newer buildings. The walls were constructed from cement blocks, and fresh red paint shone in the morning sun.

"The larger of the two is the schoolhouse. All the school materials were donated last year by a Catholic-based charity in the US. We've very thankful. We also use it as the village meeting hall. The other building is where the women's cooperative operates. There is an office and a workshop. They will be so happy to get Hope's help again."

They walked between the two buildings, and the path steepened. Looking down at the ravine, Pedro extended his arm as if he were introducing a friend. "And here is our coffee. We are about to start the harvest. There is a mix of green and red cherries. Starting today, we will selectively pick the glossy red, firm ones. This means we will go through all these fields from the gate all the way to over there." He pointed across the ravine toward the lake. "We have a total of twenty-six acres to harvest."

Jack recalled his family's fall trips across the Washington Cascades to pick apples. The hours spent up a ladder reaching for that perfect apple. The dry heat of Atitlan closely resembled the high desert heat of Wenatchee. "You'll have to show me how to pick them. I've only picked apples."

"I'll get the others to show you later. You'll probably need to learn a song or two as well," Pedro said, chuckling. "Now let me show you how the coffee is processed."

He led the way uphill. The sun was still low in the eastern sky, yet sweat was already beginning to drip down Jack and collect in the small of his back. He longed for Hope's red bandanna.

They passed the casa patronal. "This is the former patron's house."

"Yes, Isabella told us."

"It's a daily reminder of the terrible wrongs of the past." He kicked one of the fallen bricks with his boot. The brick crumbled into pieces. "The more it rots, the closer we feel to a better future."

"Over here is where the coffee process continues," Pedro said, leading him to the wide trough that ran along one side of the large, flat concrete square they had seen earlier. "After harvesting all the cherries, we drop them into this trough filled with water. We then open this wooden gate so that a small crack forms in the floor of the trough. This is how we separate the ripe beans from the overripe, underdeveloped beans. The ripe beans sink because they are denser and make it through the opening."

"Once the beans are separated, we begin a process called pulping. Follow me." Pedro crossed the square and pulled a ring of keys from his back pocket to unlock one of the doors. Leaning over, he grabbed the door and slid it open. It got caught briefly, and Jack stepped in to help Pedro drag it along its way. Inside the warehouse, a large industrial-sized machine sat quietly. Its metallic finish, although faded, had recently been washed. "This is our prize possession: a depulping machine. We take the ripe cherries and drop them into this machine. An internal screen is used to break the pulp of the cherry and allow the seeds to wash through."

"What happens when the electricity isn't working?" Jack inquired.

"Very good question. It happens often." Pedro grinned and disappeared behind the machine. He returned with a large object with a bucket at the top that fed a circular grater. The grater was rotated by a handle. "Then we haul these out. These are our hand pulpers. This is how I did it growing up. And this is why my hand looks like this." He turned his right hand over, revealing raised scars along multiple knuckles.

"The depulping machine only removes the first layer of skin around the coffee bean. There is still a paper-like parchment substance and mucilage around the bean. This is where fermentation comes in. We drop the beans into fermentation tanks like these." Pedro pointed to several large coffin-sized wooden containers leaning against the back wall. "These tanks are filled with water that triggers the fermentation process. After about twenty-four hours, a combination of the parchment and mucilage are removed naturally."

Pedro walked back to the concrete square. "Finally, we take the beans and dry them on the patios. It usually takes about a week. From there, it is ready to be bagged and later roasted. Here at Nuevo Amanecer, we stop our process at the bagging stage because we have no roaster on the premises. And that's it."

Jack sat down on the wall surrounding the patio. "I never really considered how much hard work goes into a cup of coffee. You have much to be proud of."

Pedro joined him. "Thank you. It hasn't been easy. I just got back from the capital."

"Yes, Isabella told us."

"I'm trying to find a new exporter for our coffee. I'm getting squeezed too much." He looked out across the patio, his jaw clenched. "We have all come too far to fail."

A group of children sprinted across the patio. A toddler dragging a blanket tried to keep up. A flock of green birds scattered from a shade tree across the way. Jack didn't need to look over. A lifetime of thoughts fluttered through the man next to him. He wanted to offer to help, but he recognized Pedro as a man who sensed an empty promise before it was even made.

Pedro exhaled deeply. "Shall we get some lunch?"

"Let's do that."

After lunch, Jack met Pedro back at the coffee patio. He looked at Jack's feet. "You going to wear those?"

Jack looked down at his flip-flops. "These won't work?"

"It will be very difficult standing in the steep ravine."

"I can run back and get some tennis shoes." He jogged back to his home, passing the children who had paused to console the sniffling, crying toddler. Jack dug through his bag, throwing his clothes across his bed. He found socks and shoes at the bottom of his bag, slipped them on, and returned to Pedro.

"How's this?"

"Better. Now follow me. We are going to the far side of the plantation where the trees are ready."

He followed Pedro down to a trail that meandered like a tributary through the bottom of the ravine. As they reached a T, they came upon a row of full burlap coffee bags resting on a white plastic tarp. Singing echoed through the ravine. He looked around and could see no one. The trees were bellowing wistful songs.

"We pass the time by singing the songs of our ancestors. You will come to learn them." Pedro turned off the path and started climbing between the trees. "Let's hike this way and meet them."

He snaked through the trees, ducking for one branch, twisting for another. Jack tried to match his slither, but the branches were too obstinate, too stubborn. They dragged against his arms, marking his foreignness. The voices arrived from all directions as they climbed, but Jack could still not see any of the workers. To his right, a branch rustled and shook. He made out a gnarled hand. To his left, he saw the dirt-covered boot of another. The workers stripped the cherries with their hands, rapidly moving from one branch to another. Jack smelled the fragrance of fresh-cut grass and fruit. The cherries bounced down the workers' arms like pinballs and plummeted into wide, straw baskets attached by twine to leather belts.

"A canasta," Pedro explained. "Here, try this one." He picked up a belt that was lying again a tree.

Jack wrapped the belt and adjusted his canasta. "Where do I start?"

"You can start here," Pedro said, pointing to a tree thick with red cherries. "Best to work across the ravine. It will be less tiring. When you fill up the canasta, you can dump the cherries in the bags over there." Another row of burlap bags bulging with cherries leaned against the trunks of one of the tall shade trees. Two brown dogs, one a ying, the other a yang, slept at the base. A man was seated on one bag, his sombrero over his face, one arm dangling down. Jack could make out a snore with each wobble of the sombrero.

Jack faced a tree and reached for the branch. He first picked using his index finger and thumb. One cherry at a time. As his confidence grew, he used his fingers and palm. When a row of cherries appeared, he ran his hand sharply along the branch, stripping the cherries at once. He paused after each branch to see if the red on his palms was blood or simply the juice from the cherry.

He filled his first canasta with cherries and moved to the next tree. As he stepped, the canasta tipped, emptying the cherries onto the ground. He leaned down to try and catch them. The rest of the canasta emptied. The workers around him chuckled. He bent to his knees and started picking up the cherries one by one in humiliation.

A woman approached him and put her hand on his shoulder. "It's okay, it happens to all of us when we first start." She bent over to help.

He picked through the day. Ballads and conversations alternated with the rustle of branches and the melodies of songbirds. He toiled mostly alone in silence, consuming the sounds around him. He caught glimpses of the lake below as it transformed from the dancing white reflections of midday to the mellow, warm orange of late afternoon. When the sun started dropping below Volcán San Pedro, a long shadow swept across the ravine and encroached on the lake.

The workers crowded around the coffee bags. A group of them placed leather strips across their foreheads with straps that extended over their shoulders. A helper then tied a bag to the strap, and the worker disappeared down the ravine. Most of the workers were smaller than Jack; many appeared smaller than the bags they carried, yet they all marched confidently down the path.

At the base of the ravine, some workers placed the bags into wheelbarrows, while others kept walking past toward the warehouse. Jack offered to push a wheelbarrow back.

Pedro met him at the patio. "How was the first day?"

"Tiring," Jack said, reaching over his shoulder to give himself a quick massage. "But I was getting the hang of it. The fresh air felt great. Better than my office back home."

"Great, we'll be back at it early tomorrow," Pedro said. "You can tell Hope all about it, she returned a few minutes ago."

Jack removed his belt and handed it to Pedro. He walked gingerly back to his house, feeling like he'd just finished a marathon.

"I'm sore everywhere," Jack groaned, lying on his mattress. The smell of cut lumber permeated the room. Two freshly built cots held their mattresses. A battery-powered lantern cast a warm glow. Crickets were busy outside.

"I can give you a massage if you'd like," Hope offered. "Let me just finish with these drawers." A set of clear plastic bins were stacked against the wall. She emptied their bags, folded their clothes, and filled the bins.

"Look at these hands," he said, pointing his palms to Hope. "They look like I've been attacked by a cat. You didn't get any gloves, did you?"

"I'm sorry," she said, inspecting his hands. She twisted his arms. "Looks like that same cat got your forearms too."

"Haha, when's that massage coming."

"Flip over," she said, straddling him. Starting with her elbows, she worked his back.

"Oh my God, does that feel good. Can you do this every night?"

"You'll get used to it." She leaned on her forearms, placing her full body weight on his back.

"Will I?"

"You will, with a little positive attitude." She jumped off him and opened a drawer. "Here, I got you something special." She handed him a three-inch tall doll wearing a traditional Mayan dress.

"What is this?"

"It's called a worry doll. You can tell your worries to the doll and place it under your pillow. By morning, the doll will have gifted you the wisdom and knowledge to eliminate your worries."

"Seriously?"

"Fine, I'll just keep it here." She grinned and slipped it back into the top drawer. She climbed back onto Jack's back to continue the massage. She described her plans to start working in the women's cooperative starting tomorrow. She was also going to start teaching English in the school again.

Listening to Hope talk through her plans, Jack slowly drifted off to sleep. As he slipped in and out of consciousness, Hope transformed into the shape of a doll, a doll in Mayan dress.

Chapter 15

Jack raised his head and surveyed the sky. The sun was a dictator with no usurpers in sight. "Great day for a swim, huh."

"Sure is. You excited?"

"Excited to watch you show off that swimming stroke of yours," Jack said.

"No way, Jose. You're going in with me," she said, sliding her arm under his armpit, stepping forward, throwing her hip, and feigning a judo flip.

Jack leaned over, grabbed her from behind, and lifted her into the air. She swiveled on his forearms. "You'll have to try a lot better than that. Let's get out of here."

They walked through an empty finca. It was Sunday, and the villagers were away at church. After an early morning breakfast, Hope suggested they hike to the lake and cool down with a swim. After a long first week in the ravine, Jack couldn't refuse.

Leaving the finca, they reached the main road and started heading downhill. "I'm going to show you one of my favorite trails today." She turned off the road, lifted a branch, and disappeared into the bush. Jack followed.

The steep trail burrowed deep into the lofty pine forest. Well-fed vegetation nourished by the rich volcanic soil carpeted the ground. The dictator in the sky was toppled by an invading army of leaves and branches. Streaks of light broke through the canopy. A rustle and a bouncing limb marked the launching pad of a startled bird.

Jack stayed a pace or two behind Hope, admiring her tanned legs, the slight flexing in her long muscles, and how her white socks were folded perfectly above her tennis shoes. He remembered their first hike in the Cascades, up to the waterfall. Even then, he sensed he was following someone who could set him on a new course.

The difficult manual labor of the first week dissipated with each step. He tried to keep his stride even with Hope's, concentrating on dropping his shoe into her print. He noticed that he always led with his right foot when taking large steps. He would even stutter-step to keep his right foot ready. "Do you ever notice how walking in the woods brings out the little things in life?" Jack asked.

"Sometimes. But I tend to think about the bigger stuff."

"Like what?"

"Like how do we fit into the bigger picture? Are we destined to act in a certain way? Are we destined to think about being destined to act a certain way?" Hope replied.

"I... think we're on different pages." Jack chuckled. "Right now, I'm trying to figure out if I breathe through my nose or my mouth. That's the extent of my inquiry."

"Be careful back there. I wouldn't want you running into the back of me because you're so deep in thought."

"Nope," he said. "The only way I'll do that is if I can't resist looking at your legs any longer."

"Shush," Hope said, reaching back with a swipe. She began to swing her rear in a runway sashay.

"Are you tempting me?"

"Who, me? Never."

The forest soon dissolved, and they continued walking through a large tract of maize. The manicured fields felt out of place in the sea of nature. The trail eventually reentered the forest, but the alternating pattern of forest and maize fields continued until they were lakeside.

The trail dead-ended at the lake. Two perfect conical volcanoes stood at attention on the far side of the lake. Small clouds, the only clouds in the sky, rested on their summits. Deep ridges scarred their faces.

A steady wind had worked the water into whitecaps. The bushes cowered and spoke in fright. "What's the name of this afternoon wind again?" Jack asked.

"The Xocomil."

"Xocomil, huh. Winds have the coolest names, don't they? Zephyr, typhoon, even hurricane isn't bad."

"And what about williwaw?"

"Good one," Jack said. He paused and rested his hand on the trunk of a tree. "Are we actually going to swim in the water with the wind like this?"

"We can wait a bit. It will die down, anyway, later in the afternoon."

"It better."

"There will be no escaping your teacher's wrath, Jack. Whitecaps or no whitecaps, we're jumping in."

They walked a few hundred more meters, and the trail T-boned at a cliff. They turned right and hugged the lake. Hope pointed her finger like a hunter spaniel at a small, bare peninsula jutting into the water. "That's our swimming hole over there."

"Are those rocks?" Jack asked, detecting some gray forms strewn across the peninsula.

"They're massive igneous boulders from the eruption of San Pedro. I love hopping between them like Frogger."

When they reached the peninsula, Hope turned to Jack. "This is where the fun begins." She leaped onto the first boulder, bounced to the second, sprang to the third, slipped briefly and Irish-jigged to catch herself, and continued to the fourth. Gravity couldn't contain her.

"Hey Billy goat, could you wait up?" Jack hollered, scaling the first boulder.

"Come on, we've got some swimming to do," she said.

He jumped to the second, fell to the third, and tumbled onto the fourth. His momentum nearly sent him past the waiting Hope. He corkscrewed both hands in the air and maintained his balance.

"Not too limber on your feet, huh?"

"Can you tell?"

Hope continued leapfrogging until the boulders tumbled into the depths of the lake. They surveyed the boulders, looking for the right mix of size, angle, and exposure.

"I usually like that one. But, with the two of us, we should…"

Jack interrupted, pointing to a large, horizontal boulder on the water's edge situated out of the wind. "Choose that one."

They stepped over to the boulder and removed their shoes. Jack stripped off his sweaty shirt and dropped it on a towel he had placed on the surface. Hope did the same and emerged from her clothes in a purple bikini. Jack dipped his toes into the water.

"Not bad at all," Jack remarked.

"Nothing like home, huh?"

"Not even close."

"Where should we start?"

"You tell me, teach."

"Hm," Hope said, facing the water. "There's really only one way in my book. How about I jump in, and you follow?"

Before he could suggest a more measured approach, she dove, piercing the water with her extended arms. A large bubble hiccuped on the surface as her body, a purple torpedo, streaked below the water until she twisted back toward the shore. She popped her head out of the water. Her hair, now all brown, lay flat on her skull.

"Feels great. Come on in."

Jack rose. The wind seemed to pick up. The ruffled water delivered ripples toward him, testing his fortitude. He wanted to dive like Hope, but he knew what would happen. It had happened before.

During his freshman year of high school, he was at the country club swimming pool on a perfect summer day. He checked both directions to ensure no one was looking, paying special attention to the lifeguard, a senior at the same school. She wore oversized sunglasses and appeared deep into a romance novel. He dove. A loud slapping noise ricocheted off the water as his belly hit the surface. The slap echoed off the cement walls of the pool complex. When he surfaced, sleeping sunbathers had woken. The lifeguard's book was in her lap, and she was peering over the top of her sunglasses. He tried to tread water until they looked away and then paddled to the poolside. He slithered out of the pool and walked back to his towel, his head hanging.

He blamed it on fear. His head did not want to go in first. He wanted his head to be as close to the surface as possible. Even when he followed the example of the kids taking lessons and kneeled at the poolside to fall headfirst, panic hit as his head tunneled into the water. He'd arch his back quickly to get to the surface. It was always that way. And it wasn't going to be different today.

He jumped feet first. As he leaped, he felt the wind on his face, glimpsed the whitecaps in the distance.

His feet shattered the surface tension of the water. Eyes shut, he descended, taunted by the gurgling bubbles. Uncertainty barreled through his body, locking up each muscle along the way. Only his mind seemed to resist, its churn too powerful to be suppressed. He breached the surface and shook his head, repelling the water. He opened his eyes.

The distant mountains were so, so far away. Unattainable. Miles of water before him. Miles of ripples running in his direction. His panicked brain could no longer control the limbs underneath him. They flapped like a flag in a gale. He turned his head toward the shore.

When he spun, Hope was there. Her toothy smile offering relief. Something close. Something reachable. He grabbed for her outstretched hand.

"Hey there," she said, reaching for his torso to stabilize him. "Nice jump. I know the other judges gave you a ten, but I have to give you a nine. I'm part Russian."

Jack managed to smile. He cleared his nose. "Alright, you can let go."

She removed her arm, and his hands spun circles in the water, his legs kicking as if they were trying to dislodge an obstinate doorstop. His head bobbed close to the surface as he tread water.

"It's...hard...to...describe... I...just...panic," he said, overexerting himself with each underwater twist.

"That's alright. We'll figure it out. Just tread for a while," Hope said soothingly, giving him an encouraging smile.

They tread water together until Jack motioned with a jerk of the head and doggy-paddled to the shore. Rising from the water, they blanketed the rock with their towels and sat hugging their knees and looking out across the lake.

"Where do you think it came from?" Hope asked.

"What?" Jack responded as if nothing out of the ordinary just transpired.

"The fear."

"Of swimming?"

"There has to be an explanation."

"I'm not sure. Maybe it's an overly active imagination. You know, I saw *Jaws* when I was young. My mind just goes into overdrive when I'm submerged. There must be a subconscious fear that overcomes me."

"That could be it. I remember when my uncle snuck me into *Poltergeist* when I was about ten. From that day forward, the space under my bed was the cleanest in the neighborhood. There was no way I was going to let any of my dolls come alive and choke me."

"You realize you just bought me a doll, right?"

Hope waved her index finger. "Don't you dare try to put that under our bed."

"I guess we all have our monsters, don't we," Jack said.

Hope wiggled. "We do, we certainly do." She rested her forearms on her knees and stared for a moment out at the distant shore. "As for your monster, we're going to keep coming here until it's conquered."

"That's a deal," Jack said as Hope leaned back on her towel and shut her eyes.

Jack joined her. He twisted himself and let his head rest on his left hand. He eyed Hope from head to toe. She appeared to levitate over her towel. Her smooth nose collapsed when inhaling. Upon exhaling, her breath rushed through her slightly cracked mouth, rattling her lips. Her chest rose. She seemed deep in thought.

"How are you settling in?" he asked.

She kept her eyes shut. "Great, I've spent some time with the women at the cooperative. They just need fresh thinking, and I should be able to reset them on a good path.

"How 'bout you? Those massages helping?"

"They are," he said, lifting his head onto his open palms. "It's a lot different from my life back home. But it's a great workout. It's also forcing me to work on my Spanish."

"Have you had a chance to talk much with Pedro?"

"Not yet. He seems busy trying to deal with the falling prices. I wish I could be helpful, but I just don't know how."

"Give it some time, " she said.

"I will, I will," he replied. "Say, can we head into Panjachel this week? I need to check with my agent to see if they've managed to rent out my place. A little extra cash would give us some more options."

"Why wait?" she asked, sitting up. "Let's go this afternoon."

"You can't sit still, can you?" He pounced on Hope before she could respond. "I like it right here. They can wait."

The beads of water from his body sprayed across her and dripped onto her face as he hovered over her, resting praying mantis-like on his extended arms. He relaxed his arms and lowered his face to hers.

They lay sandwiched, exchanging kisses behind their blockade, protected from the wind.

Chapter 16

Jack swished his coffee around to capture any lingering grounds and brought the cup to his lips, savoring the last sip. He walked over to the plastic bins and sorted through the piles. He chose to wear the khaki cotton pants and flipped through his three shirts. Sweat stains circled each collar. He selected the gray one with the University of Gonzaga insignia and chuckled.

His T-shirt drawer in Seattle used to overflow to the point that the drawer was baby proof. There was no easy pulling. Instead, he was forced to lift the drawer out of its tracks, and only with a mighty tug would the drawer slide open. At Nuevo Amanecer, all his clothes fit snuggly into a single plastic bin.

Tucking his change of clothes under his arm, he walked to the shower. Hope had prepared a large bucket of warm water for him before leaving for the day. He stopped briefly in front of the mirror hanging by a nail on the inside of the shower. The mirror, with dimensions no larger than a notebook, only reflected portions of his face. He dipped, then raised his chin and turned from side-to-side, piecing together a full view of his face. As he dropped his chin to his chest, he looked for the second chin—it had disappeared. In its place, a beard had grown.

He finished his shower and stepped out of the building. The two dogs he had named Cheech and Chong, waited at the bottom of the doorstep. They followed him as he returned home, finished dressing, and walked into the ravine.

Peak harvest season had arrived, and the trees were bursting red. Voices cascaded up and down the valley. Seeming to have multiplied in proportion to the coffee cherries, a steady stream of workers marched past Jack as he walked. A cloud of dust kicked up from the activity lingered like fog along the path. There was busyness everywhere.

Stepping off the path, Jack ducked under the first branch, and corkscrewed around the next, surprised by his nimbleness. He climbed up the shelves to where his canasta lay from the day before. Strapping it on, he tugged at the branches like a slot machine, quickly filling the canasta with his winnings. He reached into his pockets and dropped pieces of tortilla to the ground. Cheech and Chong lapped them up. Pedro worked alongside him.

"Pedro, can you tell me more about why the coffee prices have fallen so much."

"We have competition now. Those of us in Central America used to be on our own. Recently countries in Southeast Asia, especially Vietnam, have started ramping up their coffee production. It has created a glut of coffee in the market. It's the worst in years."

"Coffee is such a major industry here. Is the government helping?"

He scoffed. "Certainly not, or at least not for us small plantations. We're on our own. And many of us are suffering. We are trying to find new ways to distinguish ourselves."

"Like what?"

"First, we are lucky to have the shade trees. They slow the coffee's maturation process and create a more flavorful cherry. This helps make a more flavorful profile. I'm trying to find exporters who appreciate this and can help us market better. But everyone is talking about this new certification called Fair Trade. I'm trying to understand more about it."

"How are you doing that?"

"On my trips to Antigua, Xela, and Guate, I meet with different organizations. It's all very cryptic, though. It's also very hard to convince the community of the benefits. We are just getting started with this finca. We've grown coffee a certain way for so many years that advocating for change is hard."

"Could I join you on your next trip?" Jack asked, eager for a change of pace.

"Certainly, I'd love to bring you along."

Several days later, Jack got off the bus in Antigua with Pedro and several others from the plantation. It had been almost two months since Jack first visited. The streets were still flush with activity. The square full of vendors. Backpackers on benches. Groups of older tourists following guides around from shop to shop. The smell of fresh tortillas in the air. The only difference was that a tall Christmas tree stood in the center of the square, marking the season.

Pedro turned off the main road into a narrow alley lined with a row of offices. Each door was a different organization and a different denomination—Catholic, Methodist, Word of God Ministries, all offering technical assistance with a side of proselytizing. They visited each office, reviewing different financing plans. He jotted down the numbers for each organization, promising to contact them after reviewing their options.

After the visits, Jack returned to the square, pulled out a notebook, and started running different calculations for the group. They watched as he scribbled across the page, his pen moving at the speed of a final exam. The sums all seemed unattainable to the group, but Jack explained the value of knowing one's options versus the uncertainty of no options. It was the first time in weeks that Jack felt like he was truly making a difference. Offering something of value to this effort.

As they left the alley and returned to the bus station, Jack saw an internet café. He told Pedro to go ahead. He would return later. He wanted to make a call home.

Jack ducked into the café. His mom picked up the phone.

"Jack, my God, it's great to hear your voice. We miss you so much."

"I miss you all as well. How is everybody?"

"Everybody is fine, we're getting ready for the holidays. When are you coming back?"

Jack bit his lip. "Yeah, Mom, I think we're going to stay down here for a bit longer."

"But Jack—"

"It's okay, Mom. We have so much to do here. Hope is busy with her teaching and helping the women's co-op. It's the middle of the coffee harvest. You wouldn't believe how hard I'm working."

"Working through the holidays? I guess that's not much different from last year."

"Funny, Mom."

"Are you eating enough? Have you lost weight?"

"I'm not gaining weight."

"Are you safe?"

"I'm safe."

"And what about your condo? Did you ever get someone to rent it?"

"That was easy, Mom. Plus, I'm able to charge more than my mortgage. That's giving us more to live on down here."

"Have you talked to anyone back at work?"

"I emailed Sarah, one of my teammates. They barely miss me. The machine keeps humming along though."

"I don't know, Jack. I really wish you were coming home. Your sisters are going to be so upset." His mother sighed heavily.

"Tell them I'm fine. Is Dad around?"

"No, he's still at the office."

"Pass on a hello. And tell him I lost that double chin. Bye, Mom. Love you."

He hung up the phone and left the café to wander the streets, inspecting that word, fine. Was he fine? He was certainly happy when he was with Hope. His Spanish was improving. The long days picking coffee in the fresh air brought him some kind of peace. But the conversation with his mom sowed doubts.

He was missing a challenge. A puzzle to decipher. He recognized he would not be content with physical labor alone. His self-worth was tangled up with a definition of success he was not finding here. Perhaps his conversations today could help. He jumped on the late bus back to Lago Atitlan.

Chapter 17

Early the next morning, Jack wandered to the warehouse, where angry voices echoed through the trees, cutting the morning peacefulness to pieces. Something was wrong. Pedro stood before the buzzing crowd, his two hands pushing the air in front of him to quiet them. Conversations stopped. He explained to the stunned faces that someone had broken into a warehouse overnight. Tools had been stolen.

Jack looked over at the warehouse. A broken padlock hung from one door.

The quiet faces became animated—they wanted to find the thief. Their anger boiled. Pedro promised to travel to the nearby village of San Marcos to report the incident to the police.

"That's not enough, Pedro. You know, the police will not be helpful. We must find these thieves ourselves," a stern voice called out. Others joined in.

"Unfortunately, you are probably right," Pedro said. "First, we must use official channels, or the police will accuse us of having our own police force. I am going to San Marcos, and when I return, I want to meet with our leaders to discuss other options."

Later in the day, Jack saw Pedro and several other men march down the path and congregate in the schoolhouse. They did not leave for hours. The sun had already set when Pedro returned to the fire outside his home. Jack and Hope were sitting by the fire, their arms outstretched over the flames.

"Do you have any ideas?" Jack asked.

"No idea. But I do know how to find out."

"How?"

"We've marked each of the tools with an NA. If we can find the tools with our name, we will have our thieves."

"What about the police, are they being helpful?" Hope asked.

"They said they would help. But as you know, they like to ignore us up here. We only hear from them when we try to exercise control. I'll give them a couple of days."

Days passed, and no progress was made. One night, Jack was restless. He alternated between sleeping formations. Hope was sound asleep next to him. Not a worry in the world. A full moon shone through their window, creating a white light in the room. Jack moved to the window, brushed aside the thin pink curtain, and breathed in the cool evening air.

Out of the corner of his eye, he saw a silhouette move through the banana leaves. He backed behind the window and peeked his head out. It was Pedro, tiptoeing silently through the banana trees.

In the morning, Pedro was absent. The next morning as well.

During the day, there was no longer singing in the trees. Jack's presence quelled every conversation , and a silence set in on the finca. During the nights, Guatemala's complexities twisted around in his head, forming knots. The vulnerability of the village to the whims of the coffee markets, a maddening mosquito in the night. He swatted and swatted but couldn't catch his target. He spent hours in the ravine trying to solve it.

One evening between sleep formations, Jack woke Hope.

"I saw Pedro sneak out the other night."

"You did? Was he alone?"

"As far as I could tell. Do you think he's okay?"

"He knows these mountains well. He knows the villagers even better. He's searching for the equipment."

"Do you think he gave up on the police?"

"I don't think he ever really expected anything from the police."

Jack rotated to his back and stared up at the ceiling. "Isn't this worrisome to you? I mean all this talk about plantations shutting down. Corrupt police. It's kind of crazy."

"Not crazy, but I understand your point. The struggles are not new. Nor is the self-reliance. They learned to look after each other. They can't rely on their government. And they certainly have reasons not to trust it," she said. "You should really talk with Pedro about what life was like before they acquired this plantation."

"I will," Jack said. "If he ever returns."

He flipped to his side. "I talked with my mom a couple of days ago."

"You did?"

"She was not happy to hear that I wasn't coming home."

"I bet." Hope faced him and reached out to run her hand through his hair. "Do you want to go home for Christmas?"

"It's the first time I thought I didn't belong here," he said. He poked her softly in the nose. "I feel out of place except when I'm right here with you."

"If you want to go, I won't stop you."

"Don't worry, I'm not going anywhere."

"I'm selfishly glad to hear that."

"Just forget that I mentioned it." He rolled to his side. "We should get some sleep."

Two days before Christmas, Pedro and a group of men returned. The clanging of the stolen equipment announced their return. The whole village rushed to the coffee patio, roaring in delight.

That evening, Jack and Hope joined Pedro and his family at an open fire outside their home. The smoke carried away the tension that had built and hung over the village. As the flames quieted to embers, Jack found himself alone with Pedro.

"I saw you the night you left."

"I know." Pedro nodded. "I saw you in the window."

"Oh, you did?"

"I'm sorry," Pedro said. "I wanted to stop but realized it was not the time to explain. I couldn't let the village down any longer. I had to go."

"It's okay, I understand," Jack said. "How did you manage to find the equipment?"

Pedro speared a stick into a coal and looked up at the treetops. "In the surrounding villages, we have close friends from the war, and they are fiercely loyal. And sometimes we need to call up these friends and ask them to share the mountain's whispers."

"Did you know them?"

"Yes," he said, shaking his head. "It is very sad. It was two young boys. Their father owns a parcel of land on the other side of San Marcos. They were doing it to help their father, who is struggling to find a buyer for his coffee."

"Will you report them to the police?"

"Turning them in will do more harm than good. The police do not understand the villagers' code. They will be punished by word of mouth. With time and good behavior, they can make amends. What is most important is finding ways to prevent this from happening again. We are trying to form a cooperative with many of the small producers in the area to pool our resources. Their father is interested, and this may help us agree faster. We all need to band together. Just like we have done for many, many years. Just in a different way."

Jack stood up and walked to a pile of sticks. "Do you mind if I add some more to the fire?"

"Go right ahead," Pedro said.

Jack picked up a stick and snapped it into pieces against a rock. He dropped it onto the fire. Sparks flared up into the sky. He sat back down on the wooden bench. "Can you tell me more about the war? Hope has told me about it. But it would mean so much more to hear it from you."

Pedro stared at the fire. "It was hard." He rubbed his index finger across his scar, following it from above his eye to his cheek. "For too many years, I barely saw my wife, and I missed Carlito's early years. I was a displaced man over those years."

He looked over the fire and up to the mountains. "The mountains here and all the way up to Chiapas in Mexico became my home. The paths in these hills were like your superhighways in the US. We spent time traveling back and forth along them. And we all walked those long miles thinking of what we left behind, but also what we were fighting to restore."

"How did you make that choice?" Jack shook his head. "It must have been so hard."

"To tell you that, it is necessary, I think, to start from the beginning."

"I was born into an educated family in Xela. My father was a successful businessman and could afford to send his sons to private schools. At school, I excelled in my studies and was an avid reader of Latin American revolutionaries, from Simon Bolivar to Che Guevara.

"By the time I was attending the University of San Carlos in Guatemala City, I wanted to find ways to create change in my country. Yet, the more I studied my history and the failures of those in power, the more I identified with those who rejected the system outright. I turned my back on the system. I thought there were no alternatives available for the oppressed in my country, and the only viable option was not evolution but revolution."

The fire crackled, and a coal jumped out onto the ground. Pedro stretched out a leg and squashed it into the earth with his boot.

"I graduated from college in 1981. The next year, the government started a systematic campaign of wiping my people from this earth. Hundreds of villages were destroyed, and hundreds of thousands of people were killed or *disappeared* as they say.

"Around that same time, I was sitting in a café in Xela, sipping a coffee and thinking about how I could help my people. I bought a *Prensa Libre* and read the headline. A new coalition group called the Unidad Revolucionaria Nacional Guatemalteca or URNG had been formed. It was an alliance between a group of disparate guerrilla groups. Something clicked at that moment. I set the paper down, walked out the door and decided I would join. But first, I needed to talk with Maria."

"Were you married then?"

"More than married," Pedro continued. "She was five months pregnant. I knew that by joining the UNRG, I may never see my love again. I told her, 'I'm walking away for you and for this.' I placed my hand on her belly. She placed her hand on mine. She didn't need to say anything.

"In those early days, I spent my time in the mountains surrounding the city drilling and planning. I earned the respect of my commanders and led a small platoon of soldiers. As my responsibilities grew, my visits home became more sporadic. The army's presence in the city was massive. There were rumors the army had become aware of my location.

"I can remember the night we finally had to run. I was on guard. A young boy came running through the trees, blazing fast. Despite the moonless night, I grabbed my rifle and aimed at the noise. When I realized it was only a boy, I dropped my gun, but the fear in his face only raised my concerns. He warned me that an informant had told him the army was planning a raid."

"So, what did you do?" Jack interjected.

"The only thing we could do. We grabbed the weapons we could. We grabbed our papers and ran deeper into the mountains. By the time we reached the ridge, we could see the soldiers' flashlights below. They were as numerous as the stars above."

"Unbelievable," Jack said.

Pedro nodded. "And frightening. I was still so young. I remember vomiting the whole night after that first encounter. The next few weeks, we moved like nomads through the mountains until eventually we were high in the Cuchumatanes, freezing at night and in chaos. Eventually, we made it into Chiapas, where we could regroup our efforts."

"Your contact with Maria was broken?"

"Yes, I could only pray she was being watched over." Pedro paused and then continued his story. "I almost gave up on everything when I learned what happened to her."

"What happened?" Jack asked.

"She lost our first child," Pedro said. "I wanted desperately to go back. To give up. But everything was so chaotic and dangerous that I knew I would never survive. So, I just kept running.

"We ended up settling in the Lacondon Jungle of Chiapas. The jungle was a difficult place to mount a revolution in Guatemala, but it was the only place where we could regroup. I remember the nights sleeping on a cotton blanket in the bare dirt, the strange sounds of the jungle around me, the sweat sticking to me like a wet sponge.

"The humidity reminded me of my trips down the Pacific slopes of Guatemala. You see, I was raised in Xela, a mountain town with crisp mornings and hot, dry days. I wasn't used to the heat. As months passed, I became accustomed to the humidity though."

"How did you know that?"

"Because after about one year in the jungle, I returned to the Cuchumatanes. It was frigid that July. Camping that night around a fire just like this," he said, pointing to the fire with his stick. "I remember how much I wished I could warm up against Maria's body."

"The next night, I did. Tiptoeing across the cobblestones of Xela, I slipped into a safe house. I covered the mouth of the sleeping guard, who wasn't more than a child Carlito's age and informed the startled guard who I was, why I was there, and asked where I could find the owner. The child answered quickly. I could already smell the urine from the boy's crotch. After learning where Maria was staying, I slipped back into the darkness of the streets.

"I found her later that evening peacefully sleeping on her cot. I stopped at the door. For a second, I regretted my decision to join the revolution. Maria woke before I could consider this regret. She held her hand over her mouth. I walked to her and held her. She dropped her head on my shoulder.

"I stayed for two nights and never left the room except to use the bathroom. Maria brought me food. We made love all day and night. I worried I would not remember her face or her nakedness. But, on that night, everything seemed clearer than it ever had before.

"Months later, I learned Maria was pregnant with Carlos. And months after that, Maria arrived in Chiapas with Carlito in hand. I stared at the child, who seemed unfazed by the jungle humidity. I asked if I could hold him. He didn't stir as I rocked him through the night, the crickets keeping us company. Liz followed three years later.

"Throughout the mid-'80s, we struggled to make headway and struggled even more to keep the loyalty of the people back home who were growing frustrated by our lack of progress and the tightening grip of the government. By the late '80s, there weren't many of the original leaders from the '60s left. My friends began to drop their swords for pens. I followed them."

"What did you do next?"

"We looked to our homeland and witnessed the rise of Indigenous rights organizations, new female voices demanding justice, and the increasing presence of the Catholic Church. Many argued our violent efforts were a waste."

A whisper broke the conversation. Hope walked up and placed her hands on Jack's shoulders. "What are you two still doing up?"

"Pedro is telling me about the war. Do you want to join?" He offered his lap. "You can sit here." She sat, and Jack wrapped his arms around her.

"What is your opinion, Pedro? Do you think it was a waste?" Jack asked.

Pedro continued, "I regret every drop of blood lost. But I felt our presence raised the curtain on the plight of our people. I also grew to understand that the times were changing again, and violence would have to make way for diplomacy and politics. I had escaped the system. We had our successes. We had our failures. In the end, we needed to find ways to return to the system and fight it from within. We couldn't keep running from our problems.

"By 1996, the Peace Accords were signed, and I returned to Guatemala with my family. As part of the Peace Accords, several villages were established where the ex-combatants could form new communities," Pedro said, waving his stick across the fire.

"And that is how we got here. We are no longer running. We are building a future— as difficult as it may feel. It is much better than it was."

As the fire died down, Jack walked back to their house. Hope was half asleep, half encompassed by Jack's arm around her shoulder.

"That was really an amazing story," he said.

Hope mumbled something.

"Do you ever feel like we are running from something here?"

Hope said nothing.

Jack carried her into their house and set her on the bed. He kissed her on the nose and tried to get ready for bed. The crickets chirped. Doubts ran through his head.

Chapter 18

"Gooooooal!" A celebratory scream reverberated through the village. High-pitched cheers followed. Jack had finished for the day and was walking up the ravine when he heard an afternoon soccer game.

He entered the quiet schoolhouse and paced around. On the chalkboard were six lines of the same sentence, "I will not bring chickens to class." The line on top was clean and legible, each of the five below a mishmash of scribbles. He smiled, wondering how Bart Simpson would do in Hope's class. A breeze lifted a pile of paper from her desk and distributed them on the floor. He picked up the scattered papers and placed them on the desk, securing the pile with a cup full of pencils. Turning to face the empty class, he tried to put himself in her shoes. The satisfaction she must feel to have those children looking up to her. He missed that attention, the team looking up to him, eager for the next step.

Another goal interrupted his thoughts and he continued to the makeshift field outside the schoolhouse. The field was marked by patches of grass struggling to grow amid running children. Goal posts stood at each side—sticks topped by burlap coffee bags. Dust billowed around the action as the ball, bursting at the seams, bounced around the pitch.

Jack sat under a banana tree, resting his weary feet in the shade. Leading one team, Hope was in her element, directing players, fearlessly joining the fray. She reared back to throw in the ball after an errant pass, oblivious to Jack's presence. Her sandy brown hair sparkled golden like a fall maple as she shoved her bangs away from her face. He was somehow jealous of her.

She received a return pass after the throw-in and dribbled down the left flank. She launched a rocket blast past Carlos, who was guarding the right post. The ball hit the coffee bag, sending the bag in flight, and the stick to the ground, a shattered scarecrow. She raced down the sideline in celebration. Noticing Jack, she veered in his direction, palm outstretched.

"You going to join us?"

"Too sore," Jack said. "I'll watch today." Hope returned to the game.

It had been four months since they arrived at Nuevo Amanecer. The harvest was ending. Trampled leaves marked the footsteps of weeks of work. The trees stripped bare pleaded for a break. With the exception of the soccer pitch, every space hosted thousands of beans laid out to dry. The village would look like a checkerboard from the sky, with red tin roofs next to the tan masses of beans. The pulping machines hummed throughout the day. The storage sheds burst with sacks of processed coffee. All of it stored, eager to find a buyer.

As the harvest was ending, Jack spent more time away from the village. Weekends alone in Antigua. Something about the town, its roving bands of tourists, its pockets of pizza and hamburger stands, and its curio shops, kept his mind wandering. Wandering away from the ravine, the routine, the worry. He used the time to call home, checking on his parents, his sisters. Pedro continued to ask for Jack's help with the Fair Trade certification, but it seemed too daunting. It would be many months and years before the certification could be achieved. Jack's timeline here felt more like weeks, sometimes only days.

The gravitational pull of one celestial body was keeping him here. She spent more time herself in Xela, helping the women's cooperative find shops to sell their wares. These times apart created fissures he was not ready to interpret. He was confused by this dependence on her. Every hour spent apart seemed to transform their time together into something more special. At the same time, the pull to his former life strangely fixated him. His expectations of himself as an adult were shattered, and he was uncertain how the pieces would come back together.

"Ow," Hope screamed suddenly. She was on the ground holding her ankle, surrounded by the children. Jack stood and ran across the pitch.

"Can you stand?" he asked.

"Not sure," she said, grimacing.

"Want to try?" He leaned down and swung her arm around his shoulder. He stood her up, catching a whiff of her familiar perspiration.

She hopped on one foot. "Oh, it's tender."

"You are done for the day, my dear." He carried her across the field as she pleaded with the children to continue, reminding them that the score was tied.

"Maybe I should have joined you earlier," she said as they sat in the shade. "Probably pushed it too much."

"Somehow that doesn't surprise me."

She started rotating her ankle. "How many days left in the harvest?"

"Pedro said we'd be done in a couple of weeks."

"I'm so impressed with how hard you've worked Jack."

"Thanks, it's been exhausting but rewarding getting a chance to know everyone. They've even learned to accept my singing—tone deaf and all."

"I'm a little jealous."

"Don't be. You are a tough act to follow. They have so much respect for you here. I was in your classroom earlier. I can only imagine what it must feel like to teach those kids and how much you must mean to them."

Hope placed her foot down and started massaging her ankle. "We haven't talked much about what you want to do next. Any ideas?"

"Not really sure."

"Want some help? I'm sure I could talk with Pedro."

"I'll figure something out."

"You sure?"

"I'm sure. Just give me time. Cut me a little slack."

"You all right?" She placed both hands on the dirt, palms down, and studied him.

"Yeah. Like I said, you are a tough act to follow. You've been comfortable here from day one. I'm getting better, but I'm still not there."

"Are you happy here?"

"I'm happy when I'm with you," he said truthfully, smiling down at her. Dripping with sweat and covered in dirt and dust, she was the prettiest thing he'd ever seen.

"And what about when you're not with me?"

He picked up a leaf from the dirt and ran his finger across it. "That is the question I'm trying to answer."

"I get it. It reminds me of a story Isabella told me recently."

"How's it go?"

"It begins with a monkey named Jose. Jose was a bit of an outcast from the other monkeys and his best friend was a colorful bird named Oscar. Oscar would sit on Jose's shoulder while Jose watched the other monkeys play with snakes and coconuts.

"One day, Jose was lucky enough to find a coconut that had fallen from a tree untouched by the other monkeys. Leaping with joy, he picked up the coconut and held it tight to his chest, yelling in delight. When Oscar landed on Jose's shoulder, Jose was already in tears. He had held the coconut too tight and squashed it, spilling all the juice onto the jungle floor. Jose cried all night.

"The next day, Jose got his second chance. He was resting on a log when he saw a snake pass by his feet. The snake hadn't noticed him. He leaped into action and grabbed the snake by its neck. He hollered again for his friend Oscar. 'Oscar, Oscar. I've caught a snake. We're going to have a new friend like the other monkeys do.' Again, when Oscar reached his friend, it was too late, the snake was strangled. Jose cried all night.

"The next day, Jose was watching the other monkeys play in the trees. Suddenly, a monkey in a nearby tree jumped in joy. He had caught a beautiful bird. It was Jose's friend Oscar. Jose cried in fright, 'Please be careful! That is my best friend. Treat him well.' But it was too late. In its excitement, the monkey accidentally tore Oscar's feathers, and Oscar fell to his death.

"The next day, a snake slithered by Jose's feet. He reached down quickly to pick it up but paused and thought about Oscar. He picked the snake up tenderly, and it became his friend. And when the next coconut fell to the jungle floor, he didn't rush to pick it up. He took his time, and the coconut was not squashed. From that day forward, Jose treated all his possessions the way he treated Oscar—with love and care—because no matter how much he wanted something, he couldn't let his excitement get the best of him."

"Are you the monkey?" Jack asked.

"Yeah, maybe," she said. "Maybe I'm guilty of getting too excited sometimes."

"You mean Oscar?"

"Oscar?"

He pointed at his chest. "Oscar the bird?"

"Yes, Oscar, I'll try not to squeeze you too tight."

"You are too sweet," Jack said, leaning over and hugging her. She stared up at him. The sun-exposed the Sahara-sandiness of her pupils, the puddle of freckles on the bridge of her nose, the tiny wrinkles on her lips, and the row of bumps on her two front teeth. She must grate them, he thought for a second as he lowered his own lips.

"If that ankle is all right, let's take another trip together when the harvest ends. It would be nice to get some alone time."

"The ankle is going to be fine. And you and I will be fine too. Right?"

"Right." He held her head to his chest, staring out at the children running back and forth across the field.

Chapter 19

"Jack, what are you thinking?" Hope asked, squinting as a spotlight of sun broke through the pines alongside the road. They were riding on the back of a Chevy truck on their way to Semuc Champey, located in the center of Guatemala. The harvest season had passed. The wet season was one major low-pressure system away.

"Nothing, nothing," Jack replied. But he was lying. His waking hours had been shadowed by his dream from the night before. He was on a city street full of pedestrians. All of them walking, reading newspapers, talking on cellphones, or searching for a space to take their next long stride. *He* was walking against the grain. *He* was late for something. As he passed, each person would look up from their business. A man bumped into him, pausing to glare at him for a moment before continuing quickly on his way. A woman grabbed his shoulder and asked him why he was going this way. Jack was turning around to find out when he woke. He spent the rest of the morning wondering what kept him running.

"How's your butt feeling?" Hope asked. "Mine is killing me."

"Like I've been riding a bull for the last two hours," Jack said.

Jack's fear of the water was also passing. Between harvesting and teaching, their escapes to the lakeside built his confidence. When he jumped in, the bubbles became quieter. When he surfaced, the shore seemed nearer, and his body danced below the surface, welcoming the resistance of the water.

When things broke down, there was Hope. *Come on Jack, I don't care if it's dark, there's plenty of moonlight to see the shore. Of course you can do it. Do it for me.* She never gave up.

When he emerged from the water, he embraced Hope tighter, warmer, more thankful. The small of her back welcomed his hands. Her vertebrae became slots for his fingers. His nose dug itself deeper into her hair.

With the coffee harvest finished, a trip to swim in the pools of Guatemala's famous waterfall, Semuc Champey, seemed like the right thing to do. A chance to show Hope how far he had come.

The truck pulled into the parking lot, and they jumped out. A winding path into the lush forest marked the way, a mist hanging in the trees hinting at the waterfall's presence. A security officer guarded the trailhead.

As they approached the officer, he extended his palm— saying nothing. Jack stood for a second. The worker still said nothing, his palm frozen.

"What do you want?" Jack asked tersely. "Is it money?"

"Five quetzales."

"Here you go," Jack said, dropping a five-quetzal note into his palm. They walked ahead.

"Five quetzal each," the officer said, putting his hand on Jack's shoulder.

Jack looked at him and was back in the dream. He wanted to throw the guard's hand off his shoulder. He knew better. He passed the five-quetzal note in his pocket and dropped four one-quetzal notes and two fifty-centavo pieces onto his palm.

"Thank you," the officer replied.

"You okay, Jack? You seem out of sorts," Hope said, rubbing his back.

"Just a bit. A nice swim may do the trick," he said optimistically.

After a long hike upriver, the pools of Semuc Champey appeared. Upriver from the pools, the Rio Cahabon poured violently through a steep gorge, its rumble seeming to shake the trees. When the water reached the pools, the river split into two worlds. Above, a set of terraced turquoise pools connected by gentle, trickling waterfalls. The pools were of varying sizes and depths. A place fit for the gods. Below the pools, the water tunneled into a natural limestone cave, a quiet rumble reminding the lighthearted trickles above of the foreboding existence below.

Hope and Jack searched for a pool. They started at the top and leaped into a smaller pool to swim in short sprints and slap water in each other's faces. They performed underwater handstands. They counted the number of underwater flips they could perform. Hope did four. Jack did one twisting rendition that Hope counted as one. Where the limestone was smooth enough, they slid down the natural slides into the pool below.

When their breathing turned to panting, they found a plateau in the middle of a large pool. The sun was directly overheard. They lay on their sides, staring at each other.

"Just like our rock back at the lake, huh," Hope said.

"Yup. Except for the privacy," Jack said, raising his head toward a security guard who paced back and forth between the pines on the far shore.

Hope grabbed Jack's chin and reoriented him toward her. She crept onto his chest, crowbarring her right leg between his legs. Her hand rested on his waist while two fingers snuck beneath his waistband. The beads of water on their body were flash-heated. Her head lifted, and their lips locked. They pretzeled tighter together.

"What about the guard?" Jack asked.

Hope didn't respond. Locking her lips tighter around Jack's, she grabbed a handful of his shorts, and pulled him down into the water. The boulder blanketed them from the prying eyes of the distant shore. The river roared in the distance.

Several splashes later, they emerged from the water to lie on the rock. Jack sprawled on his back, and Hope reached over to hold him, digging her face dug into his chest.

"You figured out what you want to do next?" she asked, the words coming out garbled.

"Not that again. I really don't know," he said, his thoughts shifting back to his dream, the uncertainty. The quiet pools above with Hope and the relentless rush below the surface tumbling his thoughts. "What about you now that the kids are on a break?"

"I'll continue helping out with the cooperative. I have the marketing seminar down in Xela coming up. There are a bunch of international organizations there, all of them looking for new ways to market artisanal work outside of Guatemala. I'll have to prepare for that."

"I still can't get over it," Jack said.

"What's that?" Hope responded.

"You teaching business skills," he said, recollecting their first conversation. "I mean, don't you remember your sermon on capitalism?"

"Of course I do," Hope said. "I converted you, didn't I."

"And tricked me, you little devil," he said, admonishing her with a tap on her freckled nose. "Look at you now."

"I'm just helping them step into the world," Hope said. "And don't you worry, I tell them to try their hardest to keep their perspective."

He stared into the sky. Seeming to sense his uneasiness, she asked, "How about we have a little swimming lesson? That will do wonders for your rambling mind."

"Don't worry about it," Jack said, "You get some sleep."

"No way. We're getting you in the water."

"Okay. Okay. What's it going be this time?"

"How about a lap to that rock and back?" She pointed to a rock about thirty meters in front of her. "That shouldn't be a problem."

"Sure." Jack rose and exhaled deeply. He rattled his arms and legs awake and dove into the water.

It was quiet below the surface. He dug his hands deeper into the water before him. The pressure around him comforting his strokes. He rose to the surface and heard Hope's cheers. He turned his head back into the water, confident of his next stroke.

But Hope's voice gurgled. The bubbles from his kicking legs ridiculed him. His arms collapsed in the air. His legs followed. There were too many moving parts. Too much noise. Water rushed into his mouth. He rose to the surface, spewing water out of his nose and mouth, coughing. He was standing in four feet of water.

"Jack, you have done this a million times," she said, her hands attached to her waist. "Come on now. Try it again."

He stood in silence, embarrassed. Brushing water from his face, he fell backward. The bubbles teased him again. They roared. They laughed. He tried to move across the water. He struggled to form a stroke. He stood.

"I just can't do it today."

"Yes, you can," Hope pleaded.

"No, I can't," Jack said, his voice rising.

"Why not?"

"Can you stop pushing me please?"

Hope's jaw dropped.

"Just stop! Please. Everything is too fast with you. This swimming, this trip, this crazy trip, and this crazy relationship. It's just too much."

Hope didn't move—her eyes turning glassy.

"Stop being the fucking monkey!"

The sun disappeared behind a solitary cloud.

Jack waded in big strides to the opposite shore, not looking back until he got there. Hope was walking up the trail.

The bus ride home was silent. The solitary cloud had recruited friends. Raindrops pelted the earth. Hope and Jack spoke only when necessary.

Jack used his hand to wipe the steamed window. He recognized the villages outside his window but still wondered where this road was taking him. Villagers stared at his white face as he passed. He saw the remnants of two mangled buses in a canyon below. The debris and exposed earth marked the path of their demise.

When they were at the gate of Nuevo Amanecer, Jack paused in his tracks.

"I'm sorry for yelling at you," he said. She was walking ahead of him, her head down.

She stopped and turned to him. "I'm sorry too."

"I'm just scared. Scared of everything changing too fast. It all seemed to come to a head under that water." he said. "I think we need a breather. I just need to sort my thoughts."

"You're probably right," she said. "I have that seminar coming up. You can have your space."

Chapter 20

Jack dragged his last french fry through a puddle of ketchup, savoring the taste of home. He grabbed his Moza—a dark Guatemalan beer that reminded him of a microbrew he could find in Seattle—and finished it. He made eye contact with the bartender and pointed to his empty bottle. The bartender followed with another Moza.

It had been over two weeks since he exploded in anger at Hope. She was in Xela for her seminar. He was in Antigua. The last bags of coffee for the season were sold at the lowest price in years. The coffee market remained bleak. The trees seemed to wilt from the anxiety in the air.

Jack explained to Pedro that he was going to stay in Antigua to relax. Earlier in the day, he made another call home. Sensing disappointment in his voice, his mom pleaded with him to come home for a visit, tempting him with the fact that his dad had tickets for opening day of the Mariners. He smelled buttered popcorn and garlic fries and could see his mom keeping score with her pencil as he and his dad dropped peanut shells at their feet. He hung the phone up with a promise to call back in a few days with an answer. He paced around Antigua's town square, circling around his future, and noticed a bar playing spring season baseball highlights.

Two beers' worth of alcohol unleashed his memories. The first beer reminded him of the initial euphoria of leaving for Guatemala, the new perspectives, the new friends, the new experiences. All of it amplified by his relationship with Hope. The other beer reminded him of the overwhelming options presented by his liberation. He struggled with his sense of independence and self-worth. Being defined by his dependence on Hope's drive was difficult. At a fork in the road, he could return to the life he knew, the nostalgia he recognized, or keep testing his boundaries, embracing uncertainty.

Sitting on a barstool, he stripped the corner of the beer label from his bottle while watching ESPN. Tourists huddled around wooden tables—friends rotating in and out of the restaurant to use the nearby Internet café.

With a guitar case in hand, a young woman walked into the bar waving at a group of people crowded around a table in the corner. She picked up a stool at the bar, carried it to a central plaza garden, and set it down. Popping open the black case, she pulled out a guitar and began to tune its strings. Her friends spun their chairs toward her.

Jack watched with anticipation. She sat on the stool, staring at a spot on the red-tiled floor in front of her, and strummed her guitar, finding the right tune. Her thick, black, wavy hair hung in front of her, some of the disheveled strands cut at bizarre angles. She wore Birkenstocks, faded blue jeans, and an Easter egg blue short-sleeved shirt. When satisfied with her tuning, she raised her head and ran her fingers through her hair. Her blue eyes scanned the tables. The bar quieted down.

"Buenos tardes. My name is Fiona Kelly. For those of you who don't know me, I work in a village near Antigua. I come here to sing and lose my voice." Chuckles bubbled up through the bar. "But I love it. The singing, that is, not the losing voice part. Well, I hope you enjoy it."

Her shirt sleeve sliced her bicep in half, and Jack watched her long, slender muscles beneath skin as smooth as the stained pine of the guitar, pulsate to the music as she fingerpicked the strings. He ordered another drink.

Her raspy voice erupted. It carried that phlegmy short-of-breathless sound that follows a long pillow fight—clear in its intensity but filtered by well-spent exhaustion.

When she finished her songs and walked to the bar, Jack knew he had to talk with her. And the beers ensured that would be the case.

"That's some good singing. When's the tour start?"

"Afraid there's no tour. But thanks."

"No, thank you. I've been missing some good music lately. I found myself singing to myself, and it just doesn't have the same appeal."

"Why? You don't sing well?"

"No, not at all. I cause traffic accidents. I clear karaoke bars. I shatter shower glass."

"Well, that's a shame. Maybe you need a coach."

"You givin' lessons?"

"Afraid not."

The bartender placed her drink—a Moza—on the bar. "So, can I buy your drink?" Jack offered.

"I don't see why not." She grabbed the neck and walked over to tip the bottle and clink Jack's beer on the bar. "Thanks a lot, Pavarotti."

"Actually, it's Jack. Pavarotti is a pseudonym. You want to take a seat?"

"I'd love to, but I need to talk with some friends. Maybe a bit later."

"Looking forward to it. I'll do some voice exercises."

"Good idea," she said, walking to a table and sitting down.

Jack returned to the TV monitor, pretending to watch the highlights. He made origami out of the beer labels collected before him. Had he just struck out? Or was the ball in the air? He wasn't sure. Looking behind him at the table where Fiona had sat, he noticed her friends looking back. He tipped his drink in a motion of nonchalance, then spun back to ESPN out of embarrassment. He ordered another drink.

An hour or so later, after Jack had memorized the baseball scores and considered every conceivable way to sit and talk with her, Fiona rose and sat next to him.

"How's it going, Pav?"

"Good. Yourself."

"Couldn't be better. No work, all play."

"And what's work."

"I work for an international relief organization."

"What kind of relief?"

"Well, mostly basic medical training."

"Are you a doctor?'

"Not quite. I'm a nurse."

"Impressive," Jack said. "How long have you been playing?"

"Nurse or guitar? I've been playing guitar for about fifteen years. I picked it up in middle school and haven't stopped since. It's been about five years for nursing."

"Well, you play the guitar damn well. The nursing, it remains to be seen."

She smirked and moved closer to him.

"You play any instruments?"

"I picked up the harmonica once, but my efforts fizzled."

"Why?"

"Just got into other things. I tend to unravel like that."

"So, are you unraveling here in Guatemala?"

He felt like he had just been kicked in the stomach. "I'm trying to do the opposite."

"And how are you trying?"

"I'm working at a village near Lago Atitlan called Nuevo Amanecer. It's owned by a community of ex-combatants from the civil war."

"Oh, I've heard of that place. And how's it going?"

"It's going. I'm keeping my head up. The slumping coffee prices are creating a daily battle between desperation and resilience."

"Especially because it is all out of their hands."

"Tell me about it. But you have to keep charging ahead, don't you."

"You do." She picked up her beer and waved to her friends. "Why don't you come meet my friends."

"Alrighty. I can do that," Jack said. Only when he stood up did he notice the extent of his wobbliness.

He followed her and picked a seat on the edge of the group of friends, introducing himself and pretending to listen to everyone's name. He fell in and out of the conversation. Some had just arrived in Guatemala. Some were on their way to other Central American countries or back to the States. He found himself drawn to the conversation about returning home.

Fiona moved around the table, chatting with friends. Jack's eyes wandered to her as she shifted. He willed her to make contact. When he locked her in sight, she returned his stare, grinned briefly, and returned to her conversation. Tequila shots were paired with their drinks. The group began to break apart.

When the bar announced last call, Jack and Fiona were the only people left at their table.

He looked across to her.

"Do you dance?" she asked.

"Sure. Are you thinking disco?"

"I could be convinced."

"Well, say no more. Grab your stuff, and let's go."

They walked through the plaza to the northern part of the city, where a disco was situated underneath a Spanish arch that spanned the street. Inside, an eclectic mix of backpackers, students, and locals surged to the blaring music beneath disco balls reflecting a kaleidoscope of colors. Sweaty dancers leaned against the bar requesting more drinks, their heads rotating intermittently to check on the status of their prey.

Fiona bounced on her feet once she set foot in the disco. As they waited at the coat check, she continued bouncing like a hand puppet, Jack's hand pressed possessively against her back. Handing her guitar case to the attendant, Fiona took Jack's hand, and they strode onto the dance floor.

Fiona smiled and tossed her head to send her shiny black waves behind her shoulders. She held Jack by both hands and backed them deeper into the mass of bodies. The music and the darkness stunned his inhibitions. The pounding beat unleashed his senses. They raised their hands in the air. Their movements restricted by the crowds, their bodies glanced off each other. At first, in calculated accidents and then in overt flirtation. Glances became embraces. Eyes locked, and lips followed.

Several dances later, they were out on the street. Jack nestled his arm around Fiona's shoulders. They found a cab, and Jack requested his hotel.

Jack opened the door to his room and let Fiona walk past him before shutting the door. The moment seemed to stretch into minutes when the door was closing—the moment when all the night's events, the conversations, the flirtations, the kisses, remained outside the door, and the moment inside became a clean slate with new rules.

Fiona walked to his bed and turned. Her arms hanging at her side. Jack reached for her hands and interlaced their fingers. They kissed and collapsed on the bed. Drunk with desire, Jack grabbed her shirt and carried it over her head and extended arms. He kissed the gentle valley between her breasts and down to her belly button, jumping over the clip of her bra. Then he stopped suddenly. To the left of her belly button was a tattoo of a dove and an ivy branch which said, Hope Springs Eternal.

Jack turned to ice and rotated himself onto the bed. The sound of the rusty mattress springs seemed to echo in the silence. He exhaled.

"Is there something wrong?" Fiona asked.

"No. No. Nothing."

"Then what is it?"

"I…I just can't do this," Jack said.

"What do you mean?"

"I think I'm too drunk or something."

"You sure? Is it something I did?"

"No, no, no. It's not you. I think I'm doing all of this for the wrong reason. It has nothing to do with you. I promise," Jack said, looking over to her. "You can go if you want to."

"I think that's a great idea." Clambering off the bed, she pulled her shirt on.

Jack fumbled through his wallet. "Here's some money for the cab."

She picked up her guitar and headed for the door, not looking back. "Don't worry. I can pay my own way."

"I'm really sorry," he hollered over the thunder of the slammed door.

Limbs outstretched to form a star, Jack fell to the bed and stared at the ceiling fan. It spun and spun and spun.

Chapter 21

He returned to Nueva Amanacer the next day. As the sun set, he grabbed a flashlight and walked to their boulder, desperate to reconnect with her. Memories were born here, and he wanted to lie down within them. The full moon reflected like a speckled egg on the waters of the lake as Jack lay on a boulder, his interlocking fingers forming a pillow.

He heard footsteps and turned toward the sound.

"Jack, is that you?" Hope's voice cut through the silence of the night.

"Yes," he replied. "My God, you scared me. I thought you were still in Xela."

"I just got back," she said.

Looming behind her, the moon blackened her features. Her details were left to his mind, his imagination, his heart—he filled them in. "I'm so glad to see you," Jack said, "How was the trip?"

"It was great. I must have really impressed them."

"I knew you would."

"I was offered a job."

"Whoa, that's a big deal." He couldn't make out her face in the shadows. The thought that he was too late, too selfish, flashed before his eyes. "And..."

"And I thought of you. I thought of the finca. And I said no. I'm not ready to leave here. I'm not ready to leave you."

"Can you come sit by me?" Jack tapped the space next to him. "I want to talk."

She took his hand, allowing him to guide her down beside him.

Staring at her face, he raised his right hand slowly and ran it through her hair. His voice cracked. "I'm sorry, Hope.

These past few weeks have been a blur. I've been nasty. I shouldn't have yelled at you."

"Oh, Jack," she said, leaning her head into his cupped hand. "Thank you. I know I can be a bit much sometimes."

"You don't need to apologize. That's what I love about you. You just keep going like an Energizer Bunny."

"Yeah, I've heard that before. I will try to get better."

He moved his left hand up to her face, holding her head. "Don't change a damn thing, you're perfect."

Hope's eyes welled up, and Jack held her close.

They fell to the ground. The night was warm, their bodies warmer, and their clothes served no purpose. Between exhaustion and elation, they stared at the stars and imagined other worlds where every night could be like this.

As they lay together, Hope turned and stared at Jack. She started saying something and stopped.

"What is it?"

"I must tell you something. Something I've never told anyone before."

"You can tell me anything, Hope."

"I have a bond with Maria that ties us together."

"What is it?"

"There's a reason why I'm always running. When I was a teenager, I…"

She paused and looked at the moon on the water, biting her lower lip.

"Go ahead, it's okay."

Tears streamed down her face. "I lost a child too."

"Oh, Hope, I'm so sorry." He pulled her to him, cradling her head against his chest to soak up her tears and her pain.

When her sobs subsided, she pulled back and looked at him with pleading eyes. "And I've been running since. I want to stop. I really want to stop. Can we stop?"

"Of course. I can't imagine a world without you."

"Jack, you promise?"

"I promise," he said. The moon cast a new light on her face as he looked at her. Every feature seemed accentuated in the light. He wanted this pureness preserved.

"We need to find something that always binds us no matter where we are in this world." He looked to the skies. "How about the North Star?"

"I can never find it," Hope said.

"It's easy. See the Big Dipper?"

"Yeah, that's the easy one," she replied, pointing to the sky.

"From the end of the Dipper's cup, make about two and a half fists, and you'll have the North Star," Jack explained, leapfrogging his fists from Hope's extended hand.

"I got it. I knew it was something like that," she said. "Now we've got our star."

Jack took a deep breath. "We do. We sure do."

They spent the night on their rock under their star.

Time slowed after that night. Every moment with Hope was a chance to see the world differently, to dream together. He cleared his mind of trepidation and embraced the uncertainty. He had found someone who understood him, and he, in turn, understood her. Things were not always perfect, he would suffer bouts of regret, fear, and longing for home. But, having been near that precipice and looking down at the crumpled, smoking buses below, he understood how to walk away, back into her arms.

Jack was a man recharged. With no harvest to keep his hands busy, he turned to his mind. He started taking trips to Guatemala City, Antigua, and Xela where he met with different coffee exporters, working backward from their demands to find a path forward for the plantation. He spent hours with a phone to his ear, using his networks in Seattle to find importers interested in sourcing new inventory. The project planner inside him awoke. Tasks, next steps, and deliverables flowed from him like water. When Hope wasn't using the schoolhouse, he met with the leaders of Nueva Amanecer. He was in front of the room again, in his element.

Meanwhile, Hope turned to the earth. She advocated for, and the plantation leaders approved, a project to convert the garden next to the casa patronal into a seed nursery. With her hands deep in the dirt, she spent endless hours planning for a future and seeding over ten thousand plants into the garden. In eighteen months, they would be transplanted into the plots. A new dawn was on its way for the village.

One night in bed, Jack pointed to their tin roof ceiling, imagining their North Star above their heads.

"Right about there."

"I don't know. I think it's right about there." She redirected his hand.

"Okay, okay," Jack said. He dropped his hand. "You know. It's been almost eight months since we got here."

"And?"

"And we've been making great headway. But I think we may be more useful up there." His hand rose again.

"Doing what?"

"I have an idea. I think we should start a non-profit back in Seattle. We could raise funds to help Pedro finance the improvements they need. If they want to expand the nursery or get a roaster, they'll need funds. We could even structure it as a social enterprise where we provide discounted loans. That would get us even more donors."

"Yes, I love it," Hope said. "I can finally use that certificate."

"That crossed my mind," Jack said, grinning.

"How fast do you expect this to happen?"

"It will be a few months, I'm sure. I don't want to rush anything, but I wanted to get your thoughts."

"I'm not going to stop you. How can I help?"

"Just keep being the energetic you. You have your hands full between school, the women's cooperative, and the nursery. I'll let you know when I need a hand."

"The monkey understands."

He punched her lightly on the shoulder. "Stop it. I happen to love that monkey."

"You're so sweet." She leaned over and pecked him on the cheek. "Should we tell Pedro and Maria?"

"Not yet, let's get our plan together." He mimed zipping his mouth shut. "It will be our little secret." He locked his lips and handed Hope the keys.

She sealed her lips. The secret was planted.

"I'll miss this place."

"Me too. But I think it's the best thing for everyone."

"You're probably right."

Chapter 22

Jack's eyes flashed open as the roof trembled from a crack of thunder. He flipped over, dug his arm into the mattress, and slipped it beneath Hope's pillow and under her shoulder. His other arm fell on her thigh. She was tense.

"What's up?" he asked.

"I don't know," she said. "I'm just antsy."

He ran his hand slowly along her thigh. "Maybe I could help with that?"

"Sorry, Jack," she replied, slipping out of bed. "I need a walk."

"In this?"

"I love walking in the thunder and lightning," she said, pulling a pair of striped sweatpants over her legs. "I'll be back in a little bit."

"Don't forget a flashlight."

She pointed a beam into his eyes. "I'm a step ahead of you."

"Of course you are," he said, doubling up his hands to defend himself from the beam.

She leaned over and kissed him on the cheek. "I'll make it up to you when I come back. I promise."

"I'll be waiting."

A lightning flash cast her shadow across the room as she grabbed her orange backpack. The room shook. She closed the door, blowing him a kiss.

He leaned onto his elbow and looked out the window to see her flashlight illuminating the forest.

He flopped onto his back and used his hands to create a pillow, his thoughts moving to their recent conversation about the non-profit. It was time to start moving from planning to executing, and he would travel back to Seattle soon. He was confident about his ability to find willing donors to get their project off the ground. Hope would remain in Nuevo Amanecer to help keep things in order.

Beyond getting the non-profit incorporated, there was another reason he wanted to return. His relationship with Hope was progressing faster than expected. A destination not even on his radar a year ago was fast approaching. And he wasn't nervous or anxious. He was ready. A trip to Seattle would allow him to find a special ring to place on Hope's finger. Nothing too fancy. He imagined himself scouring Pike Place Market for a simple, functional ring. He grinned, sighed, and grabbed Hope's pillow. He held it tight and fell asleep.

Jack woke to the morning sun cascading through the window. The bed was half-empty. He sniffed for the sweet aroma of freshly brewed coffee, checking the counter for a used coffee cup. He looked for Hope's sandals. The flashlight from last night. Nothing.

He walked half-asleep to the shower and dumped fresh, cold water over his head. He slipped on a shirt and shorts and headed to the ravine, where he mumbled his good mornings to the other villagers assembled in a clearing. A new harvest season was weeks away, and the workers were preparing for the annual cleaning of the coffee streets. Rakes would be dragged back and forth through the ravine to clear the ground for harvest. Picking up a rake, he stepped up into the trees.

"Is she back?" he asked, releasing a coffee tree branch, and moving out of its way as the branch catapulted to the sky. Maria had climbed up the hillside, oddly out of breath.

"Not yet. I came to ask you if you've seen her."

"She left early this morning for a walk. But she hasn't returned. That's really strange."

"Should we wait, or do you want one of us to go looking?"

"I'm sure she'll be back soon. Let's give her until the afternoon."

"I'm sure she'll be back too," Maria said, turning to descend the ravine. He picked up the rake and dragged it through the dirt. His movements became slower, less deliberate.

He paused to rest on the handle of the rake. Perhaps she stopped and conversed with a passerby—that wouldn't be unlike her. Perhaps the walk rejuvenated her, and she took a longer route. Perhaps she went for a swim and rested on the rock, fell asleep, and would soon be on her way back to the village. Every theory he envisioned, however, felt forced. Before lunch, he was on his way to the women's co-op building.

He stopped a couple of rows down the ravine. "Pedro, I'm going to take a break. Apparently, Hope hasn't returned from her walk. I'm going to track her down."

"Let me know if you need any help," Pedro said.

"Sure will," Jack said as he continued to the women's co-op. His legs were rubber, and the slope seemed steeper on the descent.

He entered the building. "Have you seen her yet?"

"No, we haven't," Maria said. "We're getting a little worried."

"I'm sure it's not a problem. I think I'll take a walk and see if I can find her."

"Can we help?"

"No, I'll be fine," he said. He returned to their house and started retracing the beam's path from last night into the forest. As he left the village, he heard footsteps behind him. It was Pedro.

"Jack, I'd like to come with you."

"You don't need to. I'm sure she's probably just taking her time."

"You're probably right. But I'd like to help anyway."

The two hiked into the forest, splitting up when they reached the lakeside. Pedro offered to continue walking south until he arrived at the nearby village of San Marcos. Jack walked north intent on checking the swimming hole.

He leaped to their favorite mossy rock at the boulders, expecting to see her drowsing in the sun. Nothing. He leapfrogged back and forth between the boulders, his movements becoming more harried. The blood vessels around his temple pulsated. His head felt warm. Nothing. She must be elsewhere. His instincts and his worries strangled his confidence and his optimism. He was short of breath and drenched with sweat.

He turned to continue the search, but as his eyes shifted across to the next boulder, he caught sight of something. Something out of place, tangled in weeds deep between two boulders. It was orange. He dropped to the ground before he could process anything. With his head rotated and his cheek slammed against the cool granite surface, he reached into the crack between the boulders. Stretching deeper, he pulled the object up with his fingertips. Time moved slower. He seemed to stop breathing. By the weight of the object, he knew what it was before he could turn his head.

It was Hope's orange backpack. He rifled through it and found her purse inside. The purse she bought on the streets of Xela. He checked its contents: cherry-flavored Chapstick, crumbled receipts, and sand. No money. Jack picked up the Chapstick and rested it on his lips. "Please, God," he whispered to the heavens.

He rose and surveyed the landscape. "Hope!" he screamed. "Hope!" His voice carried across the silent water. He jumped boulder to boulder, retracing his steps. *What is going on? What the fuck is going on? Maybe it's a coincidence. Maybe she lost it earlier in the day and is heading home now. It could be a coincidence. Couldn't it?* He didn't want to answer his question.

He rejoined the path and ran south toward San Marcos, needing to find Pedro.

When he arrived at the village, his shirt was soaked. He stopped his sprint at the first house. A man was standing in his doorway, wearing a white tank top, and smoking a cigarette, resting his hand on the doorframe to hold himself up. He hardly moved when he saw his sweaty visitor.

"Have you seen Pedro?"

"Pedro who?"

"Pedro..." he said. "Pedro of Nuevo Amanecer."

"He just passed by here five or ten minutes ago," he said, pointing at a road switch backing up the hill from the lake. "He walked up that way."

"Thanks," Jack said, sprinting up the hill.

The man took a long inhale of his cigarette and watched Jack ascend. "No problem," he replied. Smoke billowed around his head.

At the top of the hill, Jack saw Pedro leaving a house.

"Pedro!" he yelled. "Pedro!"

Pedro stopped in his tracks and stared down at Jack.

Jack was sprinting and shaking the bag above his head like it was a winning lotto ticket.

"I found Hope's bag down by the swimming hole."

"But no Hope?"

"No. I am afraid something bad has happened. Something really bad."

"Is that all you found?"

"Yes."

"She could have dropped it, right?"

"Right? But..."

"Don't think about it, Jack," Pedro responded. "Let's head to the police station. Maybe they can help."

A chain-link fence topped with barbwire enclosed the police station. Two Toyota pickup trucks lined the dirt driveway. Off to the left of a two-story administration building was what looked like a small dormitory. Officers crowded around the large pine door, smoking and conversing on the steps of the administration building. Several hammocks, occupied by officers, swung gently between the columns. The officers were wearing dark blue uniforms and black combat boots. Some wore sombreros. Others wore sunglasses. M-16s dug their noses into the cement and leaned against the exterior of the building. When Pedro and Jack approached them, the officers turned and stood up; out of respect or out of defense, Jack did not know.

"Gentlemen," Pedro said, "Where is Lieutenant Morales?"

"He's just inside," an older mustached officer replied nonchalantly. "What's the problem?"

"We don't know if there is a problem yet. Can you please just get the lieutenant?"

"Just a moment," the officer replied and walked inside. A gray-haired officer with a large scar across his chin and acne scars on his tan leather cheeks appeared at the doorway.

"Pedro, what brings you here?"

"I'd like to talk in private, Lieutenant."

"No problem," he said, descending the steps and walking out onto the driveway. "Who is your gringo friend?"

"This is Jack. You've probably seen him around. He has been working at the finca for the last few months."

Morales reached his hand across Pedro and shook hands with Jack. "Nice to meet you, Jack. I'm Lieutenant Morales. I oversee all the operations on this side of the lake." His outstretched right arm swept across the lake.

"Nice to meet you." Only now did he remember what he must have looked like to the police officers. His sweat-infused white shirt looked like waxed paper.

"Please take a seat," Morales said, pointing to three blue plastic chairs under a tree. "What brings you in?"

"We are missing someone. She has been gone since this morning, and Jack here found her purse emptied of its money," Pedro paused and stared at Morales. "I think it would be wise to send some officers out to look for her."

"We could do this." Morales nodded. "Was she from the village?"

"She is Jack's girlfriend, Hope Rossellini, from the US," Pedro said. "She's been working at the village as well."

Morales paused momentarily. He pursed his lips and looked at Jack. "Was she out by herself then?"

"Yes, but," Jack said, shaking his head. "Why does that matter?"

Pedro grabbed Jack. "Calm down," he said.

"Well, sir," Morales said, folding his arms. "We have to know these things. Pedro, I'll get a team together and we'll start searching the area. Do you have a photo of her?"

Jack pulled out his wallet and handed Morales a photo of Hope making a coffee behind the espresso machine at Café Escape. Her face said *I'm busy, can you just take the photo?*

Morales looked the photo over and nodded. "I'll show my officers." He stood, extended his hand to Pedro and Jack, and then returned up the station's stairs.

Jack watched as Morales tapped a group of officers on the shoulder. They grabbed their rifles, descended the stairs, and dispersed.

Maybe he is taking this seriously, Jack thought. He turned to Pedro. "What should we do?"

"I think we should return to our village and wait," Pedro said, "Who knows, she may already be there."

She was not. Instead, Jack spent the afternoon pacing around the village. He zigzagged through the cleared coffee fields. He walked to the women's co-op and saw Hope's writing on the chalkboard. He traced her writing with his fingers and looked at the chalk on his fingertip. He wiped her writing clean and returned to the village square.

He passed villagers in silence. He saw Pedro and Maria talking with others near their home. They were making sharp gestures with their hands. The nearby homes served as a shield as Jack slipped past them and hurried into the forest. He descended to the lake, retracing his steps from early in the afternoon. By dusk, his muscles were pulsating, and he could make out his shoeprints from his repeated trips back and forth to the village.

On an ascent back toward the village, he ran into Pedro.

"Where have you been?"

"I have to find her, Pedro," Jack said, exasperated. "I just have to find her."

"I know, but it's getting late."

"Can't we keep searching?"

"It won't be worthwhile, Jack. It just won't be worthwhile." Pedro placed his hand on Jack's shoulder. "I want you to know I have old friends looking for her."

Jack shrugged a shoulder and kicked a rock. He followed Pedro back to the village, remembering how Pedro's "old friends" had found the stolen equipment only months before.

That night, Jack was restless. He tossed and turned in his bed. The other half of the bed defined by her absence. It felt refrigerated without her. Her pillow seemed to take on a shape of its own. He was afraid to touch it. Too many thoughts were racing through his head, and he was unable to sleep.

In the middle of the night, he walked to the plastic bins that functioned as their dresser. He opened the top drawer and rifled through Hope's shirts. In the back corner, the worry doll lay face down. He picked it up and returned to his bed. He kissed the doll's face and slipped it under Hope's pillow.

When the first ray of sun appeared on the far wall the next morning, he made a coffee and was out the door. He went back down to the lake, up into the hills, and back to the lake again. He ascended Volcán San Pedro to the villages scattered around the lake at its summit. He imagined families going about their daily business—buying, selling, talking, walking, and embracing. He imagined Hope in one of the villages, carrying on without a worry in the world, unaware of his growing concerns.

Upon his descent, he decided to walk to San Marcos, wanting an update from Morales. The scene had changed at the police station. Officers were no longer positioned horizontally in swinging hammocks. They wore backpacks and binoculars around their necks, pacing around the yard of the police station. The playful tones replaced by nervous chatter. Two Americans—their waterproof trimmed hats and blue cotton oxford shirts giving them away—were talking to Lieutenant Morales.

When the lieutenant saw Jack approaching, he pointed through the Americans and waved Jack over.

The Americans turned. The older of the two men extended his hand. "I'm Jon Devine," he said. "I work for the US Embassy."

"Nice to meet you," Jack said. "I'm Jack O'Neill."

"I understand from Lieutenant Morales here that you are unable to locate a young woman named Hope Rossellini."

"Yes, she went out for a walk early Tuesday morning, and I haven't seen her since."

"Do you know where she went?"

"I'm assuming she went down to the lake," he answered. He pulled her purse out of his pocket and handed it to Devine. "I found this down by the lakeside the next day."

Devine unzipped the purse and rifled through it. "Jack, is there any reason she would want to disappear?"

"No," he said as a cacophony of screams, silence, and crashing rapids reminded him of their turbulent split months before. "We've had difficulties, but things have been smooth lately."

"What kind of difficulties?" Devine replied.

"You know, the typical ones," Jack said. "We've been dating for over a year. We certainly have our differences now and again. But nothing unusual."

Devine closed the zipper on Hope's purse. "Alright." He handed it to Jack. "Where were you on the night she disappeared?"

Jack gritted his teeth. "In bed, waiting for her to come home. Believe me, I wish I went with her."

"And you two live by yourself?" Devine responded.

"Yes."

"So no one else went with her that night?"

"Not that I know. Are you going to get someone to help? I'm getting really worried."

"We will, Jack," Devine said. "I just want to cover all the bases. If you can sit down with Brent here, he'll ask you some more questions, and then I'd like to talk with the lieutenant."

Jack walked with Brent to a set of white plastic chairs on the lawn. He sat down and began to outline the timeline of his stay in Guatemala. As he spoke, he watched Devine and the lieutenant examine a map on the nearby porch. Officers huddled around them. As the lieutenant pointed in different directions, groups of officers left the porch.

Brent stood up and walked back to the porch when he was finished with his questions. Jack stayed in his chair and dropped his head into his hands. Moments later, a hand fell on his shoulder. He looked up, and it was Devine's. "Jack, I want you to know that we will do everything we can to find her."

"Thanks," he said. "Is there anything else I can do?"

"Keep your mind off it," Devine responded. "I know that's easier said than done. But you'll have to trust me when I say we'll do everything possible. We've unfortunately been in this situation before."

"What do you mean?"

"Kidnappings and disappearances are a far too often occurrence in this part of the world."

"Kidnappings? Disappearances?" Jack felt sick to his stomach. "Are you kidding me? This is a nightmare." His heart started racing. His breathing heaved faster and faster.

"You all right?" Devine asked.

"I feel sick," Jack said. "Can you give me a sec?"

Devine walked away and returned to Morales. Jack bent over in the chair, closed his eyes, and took two quick breaths to try and slow down. He forced himself out of the chair.

He walked over to Devine. "I'm heading back to Nuevo Amanecer. You know where to find me."

"Get some rest Jack. There may be long days ahead of you," Devine said.

Jack wasn't sure how the days could get any longer.

He returned to Nuevo Amanecer and collapsed into a hammock. His eyelids felt heavy. He placed his left forearm across his face. Children screamed as they played soccer. A hen pecked below him. Exhausted, he dropped his right hand over the hammock and drifted to sleep.

The thunder woke him. At first, he thought he was dreaming. Was this a chance to keep her from leaving? He leaped out of the hammock then realized that the thunder had a rhythm to it. In the distance, he could make out a white object flying along the ridge. The helicopter followed the contours of the hill, circling the volcanoes and sweeping down to the lakeside. A hungry dragonfly. A search mission had truly begun.

A voice pierced the air. "Jack!" Maria hurried toward him, wearing a flour-covered apron, and holding a wooden spoon.

"Any news?"

"I'm sorry," Maria said. "We haven't heard anything."

He stared at the helicopter. "I'm so worried, Maria. This is getting worse and worse."

She placed her hand on his back. "Why don't you join us for dinner. Carlos and Elizabeth would love to play cards with you. It will keep your mind occupied."

"Will Pedro be there?" he asked. "I'd like to talk with him."

"I'm afraid not. He's left with his friends. They are leading a search party."

"Why didn't he ask me?"

"He didn't want to worry you. You need rest. Let Pedro and his friends scatter about the mountains. They have good eyes and even better ears."

He followed her back to her home and spent the evening teaching Carlos and Elizabeth how to play cribbage.

That night, he stayed on a mattress in Pedro's home, afraid to return to the memories of his house. In the morning, he traced his well-worn path to the lake. As he descended, he ran into a group of officers climbing the trail. He greeted them, and they mumbled back, their eyes fixed on their feet. Passing them, he glanced back to see one of the officers looking back at him. When their eyes met, the officer's eyes—for one brief second—spoke to him. But, before Jack could translate it, the officer had turned his head. Jack's pace quickened. His heart raced.

When he reached the lake, he was surprised to see the helicopter sitting in a clearing, its propellers seeming to sag from the weight of its heavy task. Officers crawled across the boulders near the swimming hole, looking for something. Devine and his men were there, notebooks in hand. One officer photographed the ground. A group huddled on the beach watching as another knelt to lift something out of the water. The other officers shook their heads. A young officer turned away.

Jack's walk became a jog. His jog became a sprint. The object took form. It was a body. A pale body. Wearing pants. Striped sweatpants.

He screamed. Dozens of faces turned to look at him.

He ran down the bluff, tripping on a rock and stumbling to the ground. He caught himself, but not before his left shin collided with another rock. He began to bleed. His sprinting became more desperate, wilder. An officer extended his arms to stop him. Jack sidestepped them and kept running. Everything around him became a blur. He fell to his knees. Devine grabbed his shoulder and said something, but Jack could not make it out. He swung himself loose. Devine stepped away.

Jack extended a hand to her forehead and recoiled like he had touched a hot burner. The skin was not human. It was cold. Wet. Squishy. Around her eyes, it had turned turquoise. A large gash in her scalp seeped black. Her wavy hair flattened into sharp angles. Her forearms pimpled. The skin around her fingertips had peeled back, and her nails had disappeared. He closed his eyes and extended his arm again. Resting his palm on her forehead, he used his index and middle finger to follow the contour of her nose. Water and blood bubbled from her right nostril. His finger rested on her lips. In those few seconds, a lifetime flashed and then disappeared. He rose to his feet and began to run. Away from this mess, this chaos, this death, this loss.

He ran until he reached a grassy field and collapsed on the ground, pounding the dirt, and pulling out grass. The dirt hung from the roots, begging to return to the earth. He cleared the section in front of him of all living things. He squashed the spider popping out of the ground. He swatted at the mosquitos swarming around his head. Before him was a patch of bare dirt. Life was not something he found redeeming. He dug deeper into the dirt. His forehead fell, and sought comfort in the cool earth. He kept pounding his face in the dirt.

"Jack! Jack!" Maria called. "We've been looking everywhere for you."

He stayed staring at his dirt. He didn't respond. Maria knelt, setting her hand on his head. "I'm so sorry, I'm so, so sorry."

He bit his bottom lip, feeling it start in his throat. His vision blurred. The bottom eyelids filled. Air hiccuped out of his mouth, and he sat up and fell into Maria's arms. She patted his back like an overwrought infant.

"Why? How?"

"I don't know, Jack," she said, "I don't know."

Jack dug his head deeper into Maria's chest.

Devine walked over. "I'm so sorry." He put his hand on Jack's shoulder. "I got a call from the lieutenant this morning and I thought…"

Jack pulled his head from Maria's chest. "You better find out what the hell happened," he said. "This was no fuckin' kidnapping."

"We'll find out," Devine promised. "The FBI has been invited to help with the investigation."

"I wish that had been the case from the beginning."

"Jack, I'm really sorry."

He looked up to Devine. "Just figure it out." Out of the corner of his eye, he saw Hope's body lifted into a body bag. "Can you ask them to stop? I want to say my goodbyes."

Devine yelled at the officers. They placed the body bag on the ground.

Jack got up and walked to Hope's body. The eyes of the surrounding officers followed him again.

He leaned down and kissed her on the forehead. "I love you, Hope," he whispered. "I will never forget you." He walked away.

Chapter 23

Two men hoisted the body bag into the helicopter. As it rose up into the air, the water and trees awakened in protest. Jack's long hair flopped around, whipping against his eyelashes. He squinted and watched the helicopter cross over the lake, its thumping decreasing in frequency as it disappeared over the horizon.

He turned to Maria and Pedro, who were talking to Lieutenant Morales.

"I'm going to take a walk."

"You going to be okay?" Pedro asked.

"Yeah, I just need to try to clear my head. I'll be back shortly."

"Would you like someone to go with you?" Maria asked.

"No, I'm fine. Thanks, though."

"Are you sure, my friend?" Morales asked. "I could have one of my guys walk with you."

"No, really, I'm fine. I'm just heading over there." He pointed to the peninsula in the distance. The peninsula where he spent hours with Hope basking like lizards in the sun. He turned and walked down the path.

When he reached their boulder, he stood on its edge and stared at the water. It was here that they dreamed of a future together, full of wonder, invincible, ready for anything. He could hear her encouraging him as he tried to work on his swim stroke. Her drive to help him was always there. It was something he grew to rely on.

He took a deep breath, kicked off his shoes, and threw his clothes onto a nearby bush. He jumped, diving headfirst. He pierced the water and swam deeper and deeper. The darkness and silence comforted him. He arched his back and rose to the surface—exhaling air like a sigh. At the surface, he was no longer struggling to stay afloat. He treaded. Spinning, spinning, and spinning. When his arms tired, he swam to the rock using his awkward but improved form—part doggie paddle, part proper strokes—and climbed out.

Water dripped from his body, making puddles around him as he sat on the boulder. He stared down at his calloused hand, his right knuckle scarred from a recent bout with a hand pulper. He noticed the veins popping in his forearms, his fully formed biceps. The cut on his left shin stung in the open air. He was a different person. He turned, imagining Hope lying next to him, her skin luminous with life and energy, her chest rising, an arm lazily stretching out to him, making sure he was there. He could feel the warmth of her hand on his chest. This was what he wanted to remember. No helicopter could take that spirit from him.

Jack was kicking a soccer ball across an empty drying patio with Carlos two days later when Lieutenant Morales and two officers appeared.

"Carlos," Morales said, "do you mind if we have a moment to speak with Jack?" Carlos nodded and flipped the soccer ball with his right foot up into his hand. He caught Jack's eyes briefly before turning to walk down the path to his home.

Morales pointed to a short cement wall at the edge of the patio. "You may want to take a seat over there."

"I'll be fine here," Jack said, steeling himself.

"We have an update on the investigation." Morales paused.

"And…"

"Last night, we got a lead from one of the villages across the lake, and we've apprehended two individuals."

"And…"

"And this morning, after a long night in the cell, they admitted to the killing."

Jack stumbled back, finding the cement wall. He sat, both hands holding his head in place. He stared down at the rotting coffee pulps piled against the wall.

"Why?" he asked, keeping his head down.

"They said it started as a robbery, but there was a struggle. She fell down and hit her head on a rock. They claimed they rushed down to her, but she was already dead. There was no pulse."

"But she was found in the lake. It doesn't make sense."

"They panicked and took her body to the lake. They weighed her down with rocks and threw her in."

He extended his open palm to Morales. "That's enough, that's enough. I don't want to hear anymore. Please go talk with Pedro. I've heard enough. Please leave me alone."

"Okay, understood," Morales said, turning to his two officers and pointing them down the path. "We can talk some more later."

"Sure," Jack said halfheartedly.

He stayed sitting on the bench. Across the patio, a group of children emerged from the trees, carrying piles of wood on their backs. Two dogs followed them. The sun was turning the sky amber, the trees yellow. He could smell smoke from woodfires drifting across the plantation. He heard crackles as the fires beckoned for more fuel. At that moment, he understood there would be no later. His time here was at its end.

He later learned from Pedro that both men were respected in their communities. They had lost their jobs at a coffee plantation that had closed in the face of plummeting coffee prices. There was no work to be found. There were families to feed. The final domino fell.

He had no desire to confront the killers. He knew the wheels of justice would begin to roll, and he wanted to exercise faith that they would be prosecuted. His energy needed to be redirected elsewhere. Without Hope, he did not have the heart to keep fighting here. He needed to return. Hope's body was already on its way, and he wanted to catch up.

The following day, he reached down below his bed and slid the backpack across the concrete floor. He walked to the plastic bin holding his clothes, and began to pack. But he stopped in his tracks. Next to his bin lay her clothes.

Untouched for days, each layer a memory. The earth-toned yellow T-shirt from their trip to Semuc Champey. The blue blouse with white polka dots from their trip to Xela. The purple bikini. And, on the bottom, the midnight black hooded sweatshirt, the shirt she wore on the day they left Seattle. He quickly finished packing his bag and propped it against the wall.

A knock interrupted his thoughts. "Jack," Elizabeth said, "Mom has breakfast ready for you."

"Sorry, just need a bit," he said and paused to survey the room. Its emptiness filled with memories. He walked to the bed, reached under Hope's pillow, and grabbed the worry doll. He stuffed it in his bag.

He watched as Carlos and Elizabeth devoured their eggs and tortillas at breakfast. Maria sat quietly over her woodfire, poking it with a long stick. She looked over at Jack. Pedro walked into the house to sit quietly at the table.

Jack waited for the kids to finish their meals. They slurped the last of the milk from their plastic teacups, thanked their mom, and fled the home. Their voices merged with the chorus of children playing outside in the early morning sun.

"I think it's time I return, Pedro," Jack said. "I need to go home and see my family."

Pedro nodded. "We understand. You will be missed."

"I will miss this place."

"And thank you for what you have done for us."

"We tried. We really tried." He shoved a hand across one side of his mouth, trying to hold back the tears. "It's not ending the way I wanted, but my time here with you will always be cherished."

Maria stirred the fire. "I pray you will come visit us again someday."

"I will return," he said, not confident of his answer.

Maria placed a plate of food on the table. "You eat your breakfast, and then I will ask the kids to help you pack."

"I've thought about that too. And I don't think I'll need help. I'm going to leave most of my clothes here. Along with

Hope's. It won't be long before the kids can use them. And, in some small way, it will keep us connected."

Later that afternoon, he walked one last time through the cement-block houses, past the men working on the machines in the shed, through the banana grove, the chickens still scurrying around him, and past the coffee tree saplings sprouting in the nursery. He reached the wrought iron gate where Pedro and his family stood huddled together, the rest of the village crowded behind them. One by one, he hugged Carlos, then Elizabeth, then Maria. He shook hands with Pedro. Pedro stepped forward, patting him on the back. Cheech and Chong walked up to him. They bowed their heads as if they knew this was a goodbye. He reached down, stroking their noses.

He turned to hug Isabella. She spoke softly in his ear. "You have grown, my friend. Sorrow sacrifices part of you. But sorrow also gives birth to wisdom."

"Thank you," he said, holding both of her hands and looking down into her eyes. He released one hand to wipe tears.

He turned to the rest of the village, waving goodbye, and made his way into the forest. Isabella insisted on walking him to the road.

As he waited at the road for a camionetta, a figure appeared pushing an ice cream cart up the steep hill.

The vendor drew closer. He stopped his cart and popped open the hatch. He grabbed an ice cream bar and handed it to Jack.

"I know your story. I am sorry on behalf of our people."

Jack offered payment, but the man softly swatted away his hand.

The man closed the hatch and gathered his feet behind the cart. He leaned down and, with a push, continued up the hill.

PART III

Chapter 24

The plane jockeyed for position on the runway as Jack rummaged through the seat pocket and picked up the airline magazine. He flipped through pages, catching only pictures, too distracted for words. Across the aisle, a couple adorned in matching straw hats and sunglasses held hands. The man bent over, kissed his partner on the cheek, and whispered something in her ear. She grinned, and they held their hands tighter and leaned back into their seats. Their chests rose in tandem. Jack flipped faster through the magazine, only feeling the edges of the paper. He looked out the window as the pages rustled in his lap.

He remembered the morning she woke and kissed him on the cheek before leaving for her walk. He had turned over and hugged the still-warm pillow. In that moment, years of searching, hunting, and waiting for contentment were eclipsed by what he had found with her. The future felt attainable, tangible, and enjoyable. And this future was melding together with her.

Then, it shattered. The turbulence on the flight back to Seattle scattered the remaining pieces. Denial mixed with regret. Anger blended with uncertainty. Guilt wrestled with shock. He staggered through the stages of grief like a drunkard, unsure of the ground below and the destination ahead.

When the plane landed, he walked zombie-like through the concourse, the world around him numb to his pain and loss. The line snaked around the corner at Café Escape. He looked away, unable to process the memories. His steps grew heavier. He passed the familiar lonely sign with the placard reminding him that there was no return beyond this point.

The frosted sliding glass doors opened into the main terminal, his mother and two sisters sprinting to him with arms outstretched as if he was collapsing and they were running to catch him. The emotions bubbled up inside him, and he erupted in tears. The hug grew tighter when his dad joined them, magically stretching his arms around the four of them. The tears cascaded down onto his mom's shoulder. No one paused to wipe them.

Jack stood, leaned back, and looked his family in the eyes. "I should probably change," he said, sniffling and wiping the tears with his index finger. He pointed to his T-shirt, shorts, and flip-flops and then to the winter parkas of his family.

"Let's get you home first," his mother said, leading her family to the exit. Chilly air rushed into the terminal as they left.

"Brr," Jack said, feeling the tears cool on his face. "Yeah, I definitely need to change."

At his parents' home in the suburbs east of Seattle, he retreated to the comforts of his childhood memories, isolating himself in his room. Apart from the boxes piled in the corners, his parents had left his room untouched. He burrowed deeply into the twin bed he left over a decade ago. He dusted off old yearbooks, Topps baseball card collections, and sports trophies. Each discovery was a way to forge some memory, some connection, to certainty. With his world tossed into chaos, these mementos somehow brought him closer to Hope. They were events, hobbies that existed, and by reviving them, he found pockets of promise of some kind of normalcy. A future where he could connect with his memories of Hope. But these pockets were short-lived. Jack spent hour upon hour tossing and turning in bed, tightening his grip on his pillow, pleading for answers. All this angst climaxed as the first week back in Seattle ended and Hope's funeral arrived.

His parents offered to travel to Sacramento with him, but he refused. Even with the sadness overcoming him, he wanted to face this on his own, alone. He was ready to take a step toward the memory of her. So, eight days after arriving in a tattered T-shirt and flip-flops, Jack returned to Sea-Tac, dressed as if he were heading to an executive meeting at Agora.

Jack was one of the last mourners at the funeral. He had arrived early but sat in the rental car, tapping his leg, unsure if he was up to the task. He placed the keys in the ignition, the radio turned on. A snowstorm was headed toward the Sierras. He ran his hands through his hair, closed his eyes, and leaned his head back. When he opened his eyes, Hope looked down at him from someplace above. She was shaking her head, a smile framing a plea. *Just go see them, Jack. Do it for me.*

"I know, I know," he said, pulling the keys from the ignition. He gently closed the car door, took a deep breath, and stepped to the sidewalk.

The funeral was held at a Lutheran church near Land Park. The church was nestled in a grove of valley oaks, leafless in winter. Their labyrinth of branches suggesting the many paths ahead. A crowd slowly marched into the church. Inside, there were too many young people for a funeral. They milled around awkwardly, leaning against walls, huddling in corners. Out of their element, the scene felt more like a middle school dance than a funeral. Some of the mourners crowded around a collage—Hope in a red cap and gown, Hope screaming in Santa's lap, Hope riding a banana bike down a street, leaves whirling alongside her.

Eyes wandered toward him and conversations halted as he made a beeline for the sanctuary and slid quietly into the last row of pews. In the front row, mourners leaned down to hug a slender woman whose sandy brown hair was streaked with gray hair. As he watched the woman who was certainly Hope's mom, Jack realized he was catching a physical glimpse of a lost future.

He considered joining the crowd to offer his condolences, but he froze. This was more real than the memories he tossed around in his head over the last few days in the safe confines of his room. He could not stir himself to interact with the flesh and blood of what was lost. So, he stayed planted while the service began.

By the time it had finished, Jack had steeled himself to meet her. As the last of the crowd emptied out of the sanctuary, she thanked the pastor, and they walked together down the aisle.

"Ms. Rossellini," Jack said, stepping from his own sanctuary in the last row. "Jack O'Neill."

"Oh, Jack," Hope's mom said, breaking away from the pastor to hug him warmly.

He dropped his chin on her shoulder, tears welling in his eyes. "I'm so, so sorry."

"She said so much about you, Jack. She was telling me all about your plans. She just seemed so happy."

"I know, I know," Jack said, shaking his head. "We both were."

"Are you planning on attending the reception?" she asked. "I'd love to have you there."

"Certainly," Jack responded. "But first, I need to get some fresh air. I think I'll go for a walk."

"Please do, Jack," she said. "I'll see you later. Thank you again for being here."

Outside the church he walked toward Land Park. He passed the playgrounds, the baseball fields, the picnic tables. As he meandered, he discovered some kind of comfort in forming memories that he did not experience, but could imagine, own, and repurpose for what he needed in this moment. One lap around the park became another, and he resolved to do more of this. This walking must have been what Hope would do on those many mornings while he stayed in bed. He realized that the very act of walking was a connection to her.

He stayed briefly at the gathering that evening, avoiding eye contact with the mourners who seemed more in their element with drinks in hand. He found Hope's mom sitting on a sofa. Promising to stay in touch, he embraced her and walked out with new resolve. What that was, was undefined, but the intention was well-formed.

Chapter 25

The walk that started in Sacramento turned into a routine back in Seattle. Each winter morning, he woke early, sometimes joining his dad for a cup of coffee before he left for his office. Other times, he woke before the rest of the house, slipping into a Gore-Tex jacket and tiptoeing out the door. On some mornings, he meandered through his neighborhood, walking the same blocks repeatedly. On other days, he drove to different parks around Seattle—Green Lake, Seward Park, Golden Gardens—bundled tightly to persevere against the cold, wet mornings, his coat hood wrapped Jedi-like around his head. The bone-chilling, wet sogginess and ever-present gray broke down his defenses, and tears dripped down his cheeks. On those dark winter mornings, she was somewhere in the quiet, warm space in his hood, there to comfort him as he cried.

As the weeks passed and the mornings grew lighter, Jack started walking with his hood down and noticed more of the world around him again. Green shoots making their first appearance in the dirt. The raindrops turning gentler, seeming to massage the earth in preparation for spring. The janitor at his elementary school lining up traffic cones in the parking lot to help direct the onslaught of morning drop-offs, the homes of his childhood friends, the Johnsons and their camper van that never seemed to go camping, the Bergs and their swimming pool where he could still hear the screams of many summer parties, the Satos and their first-floor bedroom window where he snuck in on many nights to rendezvous with his high school sweetheart.

Hope was there to hear the stories of his past. She became a sounding board for what Jack would do next, listening as he volleyed different ideas in her direction. Back to Ascent?

Really Jack, after all of this? Graduate school? *So long as it's not business school please, pretty please.* Back to Nuevo Amanecer? *Do you think you could do it?* No, who am I kidding?

One spring morning, he found himself at Alki Beach after a long walk along the promenade. The sun was rising quickly, and yellow daffodils bloomed in the path between the sidewalk and the beach. He stepped delicately around the flowers and down onto the sand, walked past the dormant firepits, and found a promising scattering of skipping rocks. He picked up a rock and flung it out into Elliot Bay, where the early morning sun began to paint different shades of red across the placid waters. The first throw was a two-hopper. The second was no better. But then, on the lucky third, he landed a multi-hopper that petered out, and for one second, he felt the rock come alive, its playful skips slightly curving before ending its journey. He bent to pick another rock, digging his fingers into the sand, and caressing each rock, searching for the smoothness that foretold another journey ahead.

The smell of the salty water and sea life made its way up his wet fingers, his forearm, and directly into his nose. He looked again across the sound and watched as a white and green ferry sped silently toward Seattle. A flock of seagulls caught drafts from the boat and glided effortlessly across the stern wave, thankful for the ride. Then, an idea came to him. He had his own draft to catch. This time he didn't need to seek a memory of Hope to ask her opinion. He knew how she would answer. She had helped him get here. He was ready.

He hurried back to his car, sat down, and reached over to the glove compartment for his phone. The worry doll fell out and rolled on the floormat. It had accompanied him home, Jack never giving up on its promise.

He grabbed the doll and walked back to the beach. He found a wide piece of driftwood and set the doll on it. Placing the driftwood in the water, he kicked the piece out into the Sound. "You have served your purpose. Safe journey." The doll rocked in the gentle current.

Jack returned to his car and called his friend Scott, the wildly successful real estate agent. "Hey, Scott. Jack O'Neill here."

"It's been a while, Jack. Are you in the States? Last I heard, you dropped off the face of the earth and went to Mexico or someplace."

"Yes, I'm here in Seattle," Jack said. "And you're close. It wasn't Mexico. It was Guatemala."

"Wow, I'd love to get a drink sometime and hear about that."

"Listen Scott," Jack said, looking out from his car to the beach where he could see the driftwood making its way out into the Sound. "I'm thinking of selling my condo. Could you help?"

"You betcha," Scott replied, "the condo market is crazy hot."

"You able to meet this morning? I'm here at Alki and could stop by your office on the way back."

"We're on. How's nine-thirty?"

"Perfect. See you then."

Things moved fast from there. Seattle was well on its way to becoming an alternative to the Bay Area as a landing spot for the participants in the internet economy and a seller's market for real estate. Jack canceled his corporate leasing contract to rent his apartment and listed his condo with Scott's help.

The condo received several offers—most of them all cash—on the first day on the market. The first part of his plan was complete. The proceeds landed in his bank account in five weeks.

With the check deposited, he moved to part two and made his way to Sea-Tac Airport. This time, he had no bag in hand. No destination in mind. No regret dragging him down. It was all forward motion. A walk into a future that made sense.

He headed toward the familiar Terminal B. Next to the security screening area was a row of silver tables and chairs outside a wine shop. A well-dressed man with thinning hair slicked into place sat at one of the tables. In front of him, he held a leather portfolio, thick with well-stacked papers. On top of the portfolio was a calculator.

"Frank?" Jack asked.

"Jack," the man said, extending his hand to Jack and pointing to the empty chair. "Please sit down. Nice to meet you."

Jack sat. "Thanks for meeting with me."

"No problem. So, it sounds like you're interested in buying the place."

"I am," Jack said.

"It's been a great money-maker over the years. I'd hate to see it go. Can I ask why you're interested?"

"I met a special woman there many months ago," Jack said, taking a deep breath.

"And where is she now?"

"She died recently."

"Oh my God. That's terrible."

"It's been hard. Really hard," Jack said, looking down at the table. "But, that café of yours is where we met, and it would mean a lot to me if I could buy the business."

"Well, let's see what we can do," Frank said, setting the calculator aside and opening his portfolio. He spread bank statements, tax records, and business valuation reports across the table. "Before we get started, can I run to the café and get you a coffee."

Jack paused, having not expected the twist. "Yeah, I'll take a cup. Thanks."

"Any special requests."

"A Tropical."

"Tropical it is." Frank stood and walked down the hall. Pulling a badge from his back pocket, he buzzed a security door and disappeared behind the door.

Jack sat back in his chair. He shook his head and chuckled. "You'd be proud of me, Hope." He watched the crowds pass and waited for Frank to return.

Two cups of Tropical later, they struck a deal. Frank stacked his papers, tucking them into the portfolio, and stood. "It's been a pleasure doing business with you," he said, extending his hand again to Jack. "And I'm really sorry for your loss."

"Thanks. But this helps. This helps a lot."

"I'm going to miss Café Escape."

"We'll be here the next time you're passing through. There may be some changes brewing, though."

"And what are those, if I may ask."

"First things first. We'll be changing the name."

"To?"

"Hope's Cafe."

And just like that, part two of his plan was complete.

To complete part three, he commandeered his dad's home office. He closed the door, cleared the desk, and made his first call to Pacific Coffee Importers since leaving Guatemala.

Like clockwork, Caroline answered, "PCI, how can I help you?"

"Caroline, Jack O'Neill here."

"Jack, where have you been? We haven't received a shipment from you in months and our customers have been clamoring for your coffee. Do you have some more ready?"

"Actually, I'm no longer in Guatemala. I'm back here in Seattle, and I need your help."

"Sure thing, you've been great to us. What is it?"

"I'm a buyer now."

"Really?"

"Yep. And I need your help getting the Nuevo Amanecer beans back on the market."

"I'm happy to help with that."

"Great. When can we meet?"

Caroline and Jack met later that day. Caroline's contacts in Guatemala contacted Nuevo Amanecer's exporter, and the first beans were on their way to Seattle within weeks.

Hope's Cafe opened in time for the summer tourist rush. The Tropical remained on the menu, clearly marked as originating from Nueva Amanecer.

Jack was surprised at how easy it was to settle into the daily rhythms of the café. He arrived early each morning to provide a helping hand to the half-asleep crew. As soon as the lights flipped on and he pulled up the metal grate to open the café, passengers started to queue, and the pace stayed steady throughout the day. He enjoyed walking around the café and striking up conversations with customers. These conversations allowed his mind to wander and imagine the multitude of stories disembarking from his café. He felt Hope's presence with each story.

After sourcing the coffee from Nueva Amanecer, he steadily swapped out coffees on the menu and added new selections from war-torn regions in Rwanda, Colombia, and East Timor. He started thinking about a business plan to sell the coffee to cafés around the Seattle area. He moved out of his parents' house, emptied his storage unit again, and rented an apartment in West Seattle to be closer to the airport.

One August morning, Jack was helping pour coffee and heard a familiar voice making an order. It was Negasi. He had changed as well. He was in a suit and tie and was pulling executive luggage behind him.

"Negasi, is that you?"

"Jack?"

"Negasi!" Jack said, jumping over the counter and embracing the other man.

"What happened, man? You just disappeared from the face of the earth."

"Not quite. I just took a break."

"How did you end up here?"

"It's a long story, my friend. What can I get you?"

"Oh, I'll have a regular drip."

"Why don't you try the Tropical?"

"Whatever you say, big man."

"Do you have some time?" Jack asked an employee to make the coffee. He pointed to an empty seat. "Take a seat and tell me what you've been up to."

"I'm working for a civil engineering firm," Negasi explained. "We've got a project in Boston, so I've been traveling a lot."

"Oh dear."

"Yeah, it's a lot, man. I've been home for a short break, and now I am back on the road again."

"How's the family?"

"They are fine. But, with all this travel, I must admit—I miss them. Baby Rassa is growing so fast on me. I barely see him." He sat back, shook his head, and exhaled audibly. "Now, I know what you were complaining about during those drives."

"That is why I couldn't return. I needed to try something else."

"I know what you mean," he said, looking off into the distance and checking his watch. "This is some damn good coffee, Jack."

"Thanks, I'm glad you enjoy it."

"Unfortunately, I've got a flight to catch," Negasi said, standing up. "One last thing, you must get some Ethiopian choices up there."

"Well, I know who to call," he said.

Negasi turned and joined the crowd.

"I look forward to our next coffee. Take care, and say hi to your family," Jack said, watching Negasi run down the terminal.

While driving home, Jack turned south instead of north and headed toward the dormant volcano dominating Seattle's skyline, Mt. Rainier. The ravines grew narrower and steeper as he drove deeper into the park. The mountain appeared briefly, the alpenglow beginning to turn the glaciers pink, and the rock faces a deep purple. He found his way to a turnout before the Paradise Lodge. It was a moonless night, and the stars quickly revealed themselves like eager fireflies. He grabbed a blanket from the back of his car and lay on the warm hood staring at the sky. Douglas firs framed the stars. He found the Big Dipper and made two and a half fists to the North Star.

He sighed, pulled up his hood, and settled back to tell Hope about his day.